Kidnapped

ROBERT LOUIS STEVENSON

Adapted by Bob Blaisdell

Illustrated by Thea Kliros

DOVER PUBLICATIONS, INC.
Mineola, New York

DOVER CHILDREN'S THRIFT CLASSICS
EDITOR OF THIS VOLUME: CANDACE WARD

Copyright

Bibliographical Note

This Dover edition, first published in 1996, is a new abridgment, by Bob Blaisdell, of the work first published in 1886 by Cassell & Co., London. The illustrations, by Thea Kliros, the introductory Note and the explanatory footnotes have been specially prepared for this edition.

Library of Congress Cataloging-in-Publication Data

Stevenson, Robert Louis, 1850–1894.
    Kidnapped / Robert Louis Stevenson : adapted by Bob Blaisdell ; illustrated by Thea Kliros.
        p.   cm. — (Dover children's thrift classics)
    Summary: After being kidnapped by his villainous uncle, sixteen-year-old David Balfour escapes and becomes involved in the struggle of the Scottish highlanders against English rule.
    ISBN 0-486-29354-8 (pbk.)
    1. Scotland—History—18th century—Juvenile fiction. [1. Scotland—History—18th century—Fiction. 2. Adventure and adventurers—Fiction.] I. Blaisdell, Robert. II. Kliros, Thea, ill. III. Title. IV. Series.
PZ7.S8482Ki 1996
[Fic]—dc20
                                     96-20060
                                        CIP
                                        AC

Manufactured in the United States of America
Dover Publications, Inc., 31 East 2nd Street, Mineola, N.Y. 11501

Note

ROBERT LOUIS STEVENSON (1850–1894) was born in Edinburgh, the son of Thomas and Margaret Isabella Balfour Stevenson. For much of his life, Stevenson suffered from poor health, but his physical frailties did not dampen his enthusiasm for travel and adventure. Though Stevenson's formal education was sporadic during his early years (again, due to ill health), he was an avid reader and somewhat precocious. He eventually attended Edinburgh University to study engineering—his father's and grandfather's occupation—and later law. He never practiced either profession, but turned instead to literature.

Stevenson had been publishing his writings since he was 16, but it wasn't until his university days, when he began contributing essays to various periodicals, that he attracted critical attention. Then in 1881, with the serialized publication of *Treasure Island,* he achieved popular success. Five years later Stevenson published two of his most successful works: *The Strange Case of Dr. Jekyll and Mr. Hyde* and *Kidnapped.* Set against the backdrop of the highland uprisings of the mid-eighteenth century, the latter reveals Stevenson's fascination with Scottish history. David Balfour, the young hero of the tale, encounters several historical figures—including Alan Breck Stewart, the Jacobite rebel. In Stevenson's novel, David's loyalties to the British crown conflict with his personal relationship to Alan, an outlaw with a price on his head. As the two are pursued through the Scottish highlands, David comes to appreciate Alan's code of honor, despite their political differences.

In this abridgment, Bob Blaisdell has preserved the sense of adventure and excitement that has made Stevenson's original a classic; young and old alike will be enthralled by the romance of these highland adventures.

Contents

CHAPTER 1
I Set Off upon My Journey to the House of Shaws

I WILL BEGIN the story of my adventures with a morning early in the month of June, 1751, when I took the key for the last time out of the door of my father's house.

Mr. Campbell, the minister of Essendean, was waiting for me by the garden gate, good man! He asked me if I had breakfasted; and hearing that I had, he took my hand in both of his and clapped it kindly under his arm.

"Well, Davie lad," said he, "I will go with you as far as the river-crossing, to set you on the way.—Are you sorry to leave Essendean?"

"Why, sir," said I, "if I knew where I was going, or what was likely to become of me, I would tell you. Essendean is a good place, and I have been very happy there; but then I have never been anywhere else. My father and mother, since they are both dead, I shall be no nearer to in Essendean than in Hungary. If I had a chance to better myself where I was going, I would go with a good will."

"Ay?" said Mr. Campbell. "Very well, Davie. Then I am bound to tell your fortune; or so far as I may. When your mother was gone, and your father (the worthy man) began to sicken for his end, he gave me a certain letter, which he said was your inheritance. 'So soon,' says he, 'as I am gone, and the house is cleared out and the gear disposed of' (all which, Davie, has been done), 'give my boy this letter, and start him off to the house of Shaws, not far from Cramond. That is the place I came from,' he said, 'and it's where my boy should return. He is a steady lad,' your father said, 'and clever; and I doubt not he will arrive safe, and be well liked where he goes.' "

"The house of Shaws!" I cried. "What had my poor father to do with the house of Shaws?"

"Who can know for sure?" said Mr. Campbell. "But the name of that family, Davie boy, is the name you bear—Balfours of Shaws: an old, honest house, perchance somewhat fallen. Your father, too, was a man of learning; no man better suited to conduct school; nor had he the manners or the speech of the common schoolmaster; wealthy and well-known gentlemen had pleasure in his company. Lastly, here is the letter itself."

He gave it to me, which was addressed in these words: "To the hands of Ebenezer Balfour, Esquire, of Shaws, in his house of Shaws, these will be delivered by my son,

David Balfour." My heart was beating hard at this great prospect suddenly opening before a lad of seventeen years, the son of a poor country schoolmaster in the Forest of Ettrick.

"Mr. Campbell," I stammered, "and if you were in my shoes, would you go?"

"Surely," said the minister. "A strong lad like you should get to Cramond (which is near Edinburgh) in two days of walk. If the worst came to the worst, and your high relations should send you from their door, you can but walk the two days back again. Davie laddie, I mean to set you on guard against the dangers of the world."

Here he sat down upon a big boulder under a tree near the path. With uplifted forefinger, he urged me to be constant in my prayers and reading of the Bible. That done, he drew a picture of the great house that I was bound to, and how I should conduct myself with the people who lived there.

"Bear this in mind, that, though well born, you have had a country upbringing. Don't shame us, Davie, don't shame us! In that great house, with all those servants, show yourself as quick at understanding as any. As for the lord of the house—remember he's the lord. It's a pleasure to obey a lord; or should be, to the young."

"Well, sir," said I, "I'll promise you I'll try to make it so."

"Very well said," replied Mr. Campbell. "And now I come to the little packet for you which contains four things." He tugged it, as he spoke, from the pocket of his coat. "Of these four things, the first is your legal due: the little money for your father's books and furnishings, which I have bought. The other three are gifts that Mrs. Campbell and myself would like you to accept. The first is but a drop of water in the sea; it'll help you but a step, and vanish in the morning—a shilling piece. The second, which is flat and square and written upon, will stand by you through life—

directions for making Lilly of the Valley Water, good for the body and the brain. And as for the last, which is cubical, that'll see you into a better land—a Bible."

With those words he got upon his feet, took off his hat, and prayed a little while aloud for a young man setting out into the world; then suddenly took me in his arms and embraced me; then held me at arm's length, looking at me with his face all working with sorrow; and then whipped about, and crying goodbye to me, set off backward by the way that we had come at a sort of jogging run. I watched him as long as he was in sight; and he never stopped hurrying, nor once looked back.

I then got my bundle on my staff's end and set out over the ford and up the hill upon the farther side; till, just as I came on the green road running wide through the heather, I took my last look of Kirk Essendean, the trees about the family home, and the big trees in the churchyard where my father and my mother lay.

In the morning of the second day, coming to the top of a hill, I saw all the country fall away before me down to the sea; and in the midst of this slope, on a long ridge, the city of Edinburgh. Soon after, I came by a house where a shepherd lived, and got a rough direction for the neighbourhood of Cramond.

A little while later, and I was told I was in Cramond parish, and began to ask for the house of Shaws. It was a name that seemed to surprise those of whom I asked the way. At first I thought the plainness of my appearance, in my dusty country clothes, compared poorly to the greatness of the place to which I was bound. But after two or three had given me the same look and the same answer, I began to take it in my head there was something strange about the Shaws itself.

So, upon spying an honest fellow coming along a lane on his cart, I asked him if he had ever heard of a house they called the house of Shaws.

He stopped the cart and looked at me, like the others.

"Ay," said he. "What for?"

"It's a great house?"

"The house is big."

"Ay," said I, "but the folk that are in it?"

"Folk?" cried he. "Are ye daft? There's no folk there—to call folk."

"What?" said I; "not Mr. Ebenezer?"

"Ay," said the man; "there's the lord, to be sure, if it's him you're wanting. What'll be your business, mannie?"

"I was led to think that I would get work," I said.

"What?" cried the carter. "Well, mannie, it's none of my business, but ye seem a decent lad, and if ye'll take a word from me, ye'll keep clear of the Shaws."

What kind of a great house was this, that all the parish should start and stare to be asked the way to it? Or what sort of a gentleman, that his bad character should be famous? If an hour's walking would have brought me back to Essendean, I would have left my adventure then and there, and returned to Mr. Campbell's. But little as I liked the sound of what I heard, and slow as I began to travel, I

still kept asking my way and still kept advancing.

It was near sundown when I met a stout, sour-looking woman coming down a hill; and she, when I asked my usual question, turned sharp about, led me back to the summit she had just left, and pointed to a large building standing very bare upon a green in the bottom of the next valley. The country was pleasant round about, with low hills, and streams and woods, and the crops good; but the house itself appeared to be a kind of ruin; no road led up to it; no smoke arose from any of the chimneys; nor was there any garden. My heart sank. "That!" I cried.

"That is the house of Shaws!" she cried. "Blood built it, blood stopped the building of it; blood shall bring it down. See here!" she cried again—"I spit upon the ground, and crack my thumb at it! If you see the lord, tell him this makes the twelve hundred and nineteenth time that Jennet Clouston has called down the curse on him and his house, barn and stable!"

And the woman turned with a skip, and was gone. I stood where she left me, with my hair on end. In those days folk still believed in witches and trembled at a curse.

I sat me down and stared at the house of the Shaws. The more I looked the pleasanter that countryside appeared. At last the sun went down, and then, right up against the yellow sky, I saw a thin scroll of smoke go up; that meant a fire, and warmth, and food, and someone living there that must have lit it.

So I set forward. Soon I was standing before stone uprights, with an unroofed lodge beside them, and coats of arms upon the top. A main entrance it was plainly meant to be, but never finished; instead of gates of iron, a rickety fence. I walked past on the right-hand side of the pillars, and went wandering on towards the house.

The nearer I got to that, the drearier it appeared. It seemed like the one wing of a house that had never been finished. What should have been the inner end stood open on the upper floors, and showed against the sky with steps and stairs of uncompleted masonry. Many of the windows had no glass, and bats flew in and out.

The night had begun to fall as I got close; and in the three of the lower windows, which were very high up and narrow, and well barred, the changing light of a little fire began to glimmer.

Was this the place I had been coming to? Was it within these walls that I was to seek new friends and begin great fortunes? Why, in my father's house, the fire and the bright lights would show a mile away, and the door open to a beggar's knock!

I came forward, and listened, hearing someone rattling with dishes, and a little dry cough; but there was no sound of speech, and not a dog barked.

The door was a great piece of wood all studded with nails; and I lifted my hand under my jacket, and knocked once. Then I stood and waited. The house had fallen into a dead silence; a whole minute passed, and nothing stirred but the bats overhead. I knocked again, and listened. By this time my ears had grown so accustomed to the quiet that I could hear the ticking of the clock inside as it slowly counted out the seconds.

I wondered whether to run away; but anger got the upper hand, and I began to rain kicks and knocks on the door, and to shout out aloud for Mr. Balfour. I heard the cough right overhead, and jumping back and looking up, beheld a man's head in a tall nightcap, and the wide mouth of a musket, at one of the second-story windows.

"It's loaded," said a voice.

"I have come here with a letter," I said, "to Ebenezer Balfour of Shaws. Is he here?"

"Well," was the reply, "ye can put it down upon the doorstep, and be off!"

"I will do no such thing," I cried. "I will deliver it into Mr. Balfour's hands, as it was meant I should. It is a letter of introduction."

"A what?" cried the voice, sharply.

I repeated what I had said.

"Who are ye yourself?"

"They call me David Balfour."

At that, the man started, for I heard the musket rattle on the windowsill; after a long pause, he asked, "Is your father dead?"

I was so much surprised at this, that I stood staring.

"Ay," the man went on, "he's dead, no doubt; and that'll be what brings ye to my door. Well, man, I'll let ye in"; and he disappeared from the window.

CHAPTER 2
I Meet My Uncle

SOON THERE CAME a great rattling of chains and bolts, and the door was cautiously opened.

"Go into the kitchen and touch nothing," said the voice; and while he set himself to replacing the chains and bolts, I made my way forward through the dark and entered the kitchen.

The fire was fairly bright, and showed me the barest room I think I ever saw. Half-a-dozen dishes stood upon the shelves; the table was laid for supper with a bowl of porridge, a spoon, and a cup of beer. There was not another thing in that great, stone room but chests arranged

along the wall and a corner cupboard.

As soon as the last chain was up, the man rejoined me. He was a mean, stooping, narrow-shouldered, clay-faced creature; and his age might have been anything between fifty and seventy. He was long unshaved; but what most distressed me, he would neither take his eyes away from me nor look me in the face.

"Are ye hungry?" he asked. "Ye can eat that porridge?"

I said I feared it was his own supper.

"Oh," said he, "I can do fine without it. I'll take the beer, though, for it wets my throat." He drank the cup, still keeping an eye upon me as he drank; and then suddenly held out his hand. "Let's see the letter."

I told him the letter was for Mr. Balfour; not for him.

"And who do ye think I am?" said he. "Give me Alexander's letter!"

"You know my father's name?"

"It would be strange if I didn't," he returned, "for he was my brother; and little as ye seem to like either me or my house, or my porridge, I'm your uncle, Davie my man. So give us the letter and sit down and fill your stomach."

If I had been younger, I believe I would have burst into tears. As it was, I could find no words, but handed him the letter.

My uncle, stooping over the fire, turned the letter over and over in his hands.

"Do ye know what's in it?" he asked.

"You see for yourself, sir," said I, "that the seal has not been broken."

"Ay," he said, "but what brought you here?"

"To give you the letter," said I.

"No," said he, "but ye'll have had some hopes, no doubt?"

"I confess, sir," said I, "when I was told that I had rich kinsfolk, I hoped they might help me in my life. But I am no beggar. For as poor as I appear, I have friends of my own that will be happy to help me."

"Oh ho!" said Uncle Ebenezer. "So, Davie my man, your father's been long dead?"

"Three weeks, sir."

"He was a secret man, Alexander—a secret, silent man," he went on. "He never said much when he was young. He'll never have spoken much of me?"

"I never knew, sir, till you told it me yourself, that he had any brother."

"To think o' that!" said he. He hit me a smack upon the shoulder, saying, "We'll get along fine! I'm glad I let you in. And now come away to your bed."

To my surprise he lit no lamp or candle, but set forth into the dark passage, groped his way, breathing deeply, up a flight of steps, and paused before a door, which he unlocked. I begged a light to go to bed with.

"Hoot-toot!" said Uncle Ebenezer, "there's a fine moon."

"Neither moon nor star, sir, and dark as a cave," said I. "I cannot see the bed."

"Hoot-toot!" said he. "Lights in a house is a thing I don't agree with. I'm afraid of fires. Good night to ye, Davie."

And before I had time to add a further protest, he pulled the door shut, and I heard him lock me in from the outside.

The room was as cold as a well, and the bed was damp; but by good fortune I had brought up my bundle, and rolled myself in my cloak, and lay down upon the floor and fell asleep.

With the first peep of day I opened my eyes, to find myself in a great chamber, lit by three fair windows. Perhaps twenty years ago, it must have been as pleasant a room as a man could wish; but damp, dirt, disuse, and the mice and spiders had done their worst since then. Many of the window panes, besides, were broken; and indeed this was a common feature in that house.

Meanwhile the sun was shining outside; and being very cold in that miserable room, I knocked and shouted till my jailer came and let me out. In the kitchen he had lit the fire and was making the porridge. The table was laid with two bowls and two horn spoons.

"Davie, my man," said he, "I think much of the family, and I mean to do right by you. Just you give me a day or two, and as sure as sure, I'll do the right by you."

"Very well," said I. "If you want to help me, there's no doubt but I'll be glad of it, and grateful." Then I began next to say that I must have the bed and bedding aired and put to sun-dry.

"Is this my house or yours?" said he. "No, no, I didn't mean that. What's mine is yours, Davie, and what's yours is mine. Blood's thicker than water; and there's nobody but you and me that has the name." And then he rambled on about the family, and its old greatness, and his father that began to enlarge the house, and himself that stopped the building as a sinful waste; and this put it in my head to give him Jennet Clouston's message.

"The witch!" he cried. "Twelve hundred and fifteen—that's how many days it's been since I had her thrown off the land! I swear, David, I'll have her roasted before I'm done with it! A witch—I'll go make a legal complaint against her."

And with that he opened a chest, and got out a very old blue coat, and a good hat. These he threw on, and taking a staff from the cupboard, locked all up again, and was for setting out, when a thought stopped him.

"I can't leave you by yourself in the house," said he. "I'll have to lock you out."

"If you lock me out," I said, "it'll be the last you'll see of me in friendship."

"This is not the way to win my favor, David."

"Sir," said I, "with all respect for your age and our common blood, I do not value your favor. If you were all the family I had in the world, I wouldn't buy your liking for two pence."

Uncle Ebenezer went and looked out the window for a while. I could see him trembling and twitching, but when he turned round, he had a smile on his face.

"Well, well," said he, "we must bear and forbear. I'll not go; that's all that's to be said of it."

"Uncle Ebenezer," I said, "I can make nothing out of this. You treat me like a thief; you hate to have me in this house; you let me see it, every word and every minute: it's not possible you can like me; and as for me, I've spoken to you as I never thought to speak to any man. Why do you seek to keep me, then? Let me go back to the friends I have, and that like me!"

"No, no," he said. "I like you fine; we'll get along fine yet. Stay here quiet, there's a good lad; just you bide here quiet a bittie, and ye'll find that we agree."

"Well, sir," said I, after I had thought the matter out in silence, "I'll stay a while. It's more just I should be helped by my own blood than strangers; and if we don't get along, I'll do my best it shall be through no fault of mine."

For a day that was begun so ill, the day passed fairly well. We had the porridge cold again at noon, and hot porridge at night. He spoke but little, shooting a question at me after a long silence. In a room next door to the kitchen, where he allowed me to go, I found a great number of books, both Latin and English, in which I took great pleasure all the afternoon.

After our late meal, he sat awhile smoking.

"Davie," he said at length, "I've been thinking. There's a wee bit silver that I half promised you before you were born, promised it to your father. O, nothing legal, you understand. Well, I kept that bit of money separate—and it has grown by now to be a matter of just precisely—just exactly—" and here he paused and stumbled, "—of just exactly forty pounds—*Scots* pounds!"

The Scots pound being the same thing as an English shilling, the difference made by his second thought was considerable; I could see, besides, that the whole story was a lie. "O think again, sir! Pounds sterling, I believe!"

"That's what I said," returned my uncle: "pounds ster-

ling! And if you'll step out the door a minute, I'll get it out
for you and call you in again."

It was a dark night, with a few stars low down; and as I
stood just outside the door, I heard a moaning of wind far
off among the hills.

When I was called in again, my uncle counted out into
my hand the golden guinea pieces.

"There," said he, "that'll show you! I'm a strange man,
and strange with strangers; but my word is my bond, and
there's the proof of it."

Now, my uncle seemed so miserly that I was struck
dumb by this sudden generosity, and could find no words
in which to thank him.

"Not a word!" said he. "I want no thanks. I do my duty.
It's a pleasure to me to do the right by my brother's son."
And now he looked toward me sideways. "And see here,"
said he, "tit for tat."

I told him I was ready to return a favor. He told me that

he was growing old and a little broken, and that he would expect me to help him with the house and the small garden. I expressed my readiness to serve.

"Well," he said, "let's begin." He pulled out of his pocket a rusty key. "There," said he, "there's the key of the stair-tower at the far end of the house. You can only get into it from the outside, for that part of the house is not finished. Go in there, and up the stairs, and bring me down the chest that's at the top. There's papers in it."

"Can I have a light, sir?"

"No," said he. "No lights in my house."

"Very well, sir," said I. "Are the stairs good?"

"They're grand," said he; and then as I was going: "Keep to the wall," he added; "there's no bannisters. But the stairs are grand."

Out I went into the night. The wind was still moaning. It was darker than ever; and I had to feel along the wall, till I came to the length of the stair-tower door at the far end of the unfinished wing. I had got the key into the keyhole and had just turned it, when all of a sudden, without sound of wind or thunder, the whole sky lighted up with wild fire and went black again.

It was so dark inside, that I pushed out with foot and hand, and soon struck the wall with the one, and the lowermost round of the stair with the other. The wall, by the touch, was of fine cut stone; the steps too, though somewhat steep and narrow, were polished, and regular and solid. Minding my uncle's word about the bannisters, I kept close to the tower side, and felt my way in the pitch darkness with a beating heart.

The house of Shaws stood some five full storeys high, not counting lofts. As I advanced, it seemed to me the stairway grew airier and a bit less dark; and I was wondering what might be the cause of this change, when a second blink of the summer lightning came and went. If I did

not cry out, it was because fear had me by the throat. The flash shone in on every side through breaches in the wall, so that I seemed to be climbing up an open scaffold, but the same passing brightness showed me the steps were of unequal length, and that one of my feet rested that moment within two inches of the edge.

This was the grand stair! I thought. My uncle had sent me here, certainly to run great risks, perhaps to die. I got down upon my hands and knees; and as slowly as a snail, feeling before me every inch, and testing each step, I continued to go up the stairs. The darkness, by contrast with the flash, appeared to have deepened; nor was that all, for there was a great stir of bats in the top part of the tower, and the foul beasts, flying downwards, sometimes beat about my face and body.

The tower, I should have said, was square; and in every corner the step was made of a great stone of a different shape, to join the flights. Well, I had come close to one of these turns, when, feeling forward as usual, my hand slipped upon an edge and found nothing but emptiness beyond it. The stairs had been carried no higher; to set a stranger mounting it in the darkness was to send him straight to his death.

I turned and groped my way down again, with anger in my heart. About half-way down, the wind sprang up in a clap and shook the tower, and died again; the rain followed; and before I had reached the ground level it fell in buckets. I put out my head in the storm, and walked softly along towards the kitchen. I came in unheard, and stood and watched him. He sat with his back towards me at the table. I stepped forward, came close behind him, and suddenly clapped my two hands down upon his shoulders.

My uncle gave a kind of broken cry, flung up his arms, and tumbled to the floor like a dead man. I let him lie as he had fallen. His keys were hanging in the cupboard; and it was my plan to furnish myself with arms before my uncle should come again to his senses. I turned to the chests. The first was full of meal; the second of money-bags and papers; in the third, with many other things (for the most part clothes), I found a rusty, ugly-looking knife. This, then, I hid inside my waistcoat, and turned to my uncle.

He lay as he had fallen, all huddled, with one knee up and one arm sprawling. I got water and dashed it in his face; and with that he seemed to come a little to himself, working his mouth and fluttering his eyelids. At last he looked up and saw me, and there came into his eyes a terror.

"Come, come," said I; "sit up."

"Are you alive?" he sobbed.

"That am I," said I. "Small thanks to you!"

I set him on a chair and looked at him. I numbered over before him the points on which I wanted explanation: why he lied to me at every word; why he had given me money to which I was convinced I had no claim; and, last of all, why he had tried to kill me. He heard me all through in silence; and then, in a broken voice, begged me to let him go to bed.

"I'll tell you in the morning," he said; "as sure as death I will."

And so weak was he that I could do nothing but consent. I locked him in his room, however, and pocketed the key; and then returning to the kitchen, made up such a blaze as had not shone there for many a long year, and wrapping myself in my plaid, lay down upon the chests and fell asleep.

CHAPTER 3
I Go to the Queen's Ferry

MUCH RAIN FELL in the night; and the next morning there blew a bitter wintry wind out of the northwest, driving scattered clouds.

I went upstairs and gave my prisoner his liberty. He gave me good-morning; and I gave the same to him. Soon we were set to breakfast.

"Well, sir," said I, "have you nothing more to say to me?" And then, as he did not answer, I continued, "It will be time, I think, to understand each other. You took me for a Johnnie Raw, with no more mother-wit or courage than a porridge-stick. I took you for a good man, or no worse than others at the least. It seems we were both wrong. What cause you have to fear me, to cheat me, and to attempt my life—"

He murmured something about a joke, and that he liked a bit of fun. We were then interrupted by a knocking at the door.

Bidding my uncle sit where he was, I went to open it, and found on the doorstep a half-grown boy in sea-clothes. He had no sooner seen me than he began to dance some steps, snapping his fingers in the air.

"What cheer, mate?" said he.

I asked him to name his business, but instead he sang two lines of nonsense.

"Well," said I, "if you have no business, I will be so rude as to shut you out."

"Wait, brother!" he cried. "Have you no fun about you? Or do you want to get me thrashed? I've brought a letter from old Heasyoasy to Mr. Belflower." He showed me a letter as he spoke. "And I say, mate," he added, "I'm awful hungry."

"Well," said I, "come into the house, and you shall have a bite."

With that I brought him in and set him down to my own place, where he fell-to on the remains of breakfast. Meanwhile, my uncle read the letter and sat thinking; then, suddenly, he got to his feet and pulled me to the farthest corner of the room.

"Read that," said he, and put the letter in my hand.

> The Hawes Inn, at the Queen's Ferry.
>
> Sir,—I lie here with my hawser up and down, and send my cabin-boy to inform. If you have any further commands for overseas, today will be the last chance, as the wind will serve us well. I have disputes with your agent, Mr. Rankeillor; of which, if not cleared up, you may look to see some losses. I have drawn a bill upon you, and am, sir, your humble servant,
>
> ELIAS HOSEASON.

"You see, Davie," resumed my uncle, "I have a venture with this man Hoseason, the captain of the trading brig, the *Covenant*, of Dysart. Now, if you and me was to walk over with that lad, I could see the captain at the Hawes, or maybe on board the *Covenant* if there was papers to be signed; and so far from a loss of time, we can go on to the lawyer, Mr. Rankeillor's. After all that's come and gone, you wouldn't believe me upon my word; but you'll believe Rankeillor. He's a respected old man, and he knew your father."

I stood awhile and thought. I was going to some place of shipping, which was doubtless busy, and where my uncle would dare not attempt to harm me. Besides, I was eager to take a nearer view of the sea and ships. You are to remember that I had lived all my life in the inland hills, and just two days before had my first sight of the firth lying like a blue floor, and the sailing ships moving on the face of it, no bigger than toys.

"Very well," said I, "let us go to the Ferry."

My uncle got into his hat and coat, and buckled an old rusty sword on; then we locked the door and went out.

It was the month of June; the grass was all white with daisies, and the trees with blossom; but to judge by our blue nails and aching wrists, the time might have been winter and the whiteness a December frost. Uncle Ebenezer trudged along, never saying a word the whole way; and I was left for talk with the cabin-boy. He told me his name was Ransome, and that he had followed the sea since he was nine, but could not say how old he was, as he had lost track. He showed me tattoo marks, baring his chest; he swore horribly, more like a silly schoolboy than a man; and boasted of many wild and bad things that he had done: stealing, false accusations, ay, and even murder; but all with such a lack of likely details, as made me pity him rather than believe him.

I asked him of the brig and of Captain Hoseason. Heasyoasy (for so he named the skipper) was rough, fierce, mean, and brutal; and all this the poor cabin-boy admired as something seamanlike and manly. He would only admit one flaw in his idol. "He ain't no seaman. It's Mr. Shuan that navigates the brig; he's the finest seaman in the trade, only he drinks too much. Why, look here"; and turning down his stocking he showed me a great, raw, red wound that made my blood run cold. "He done that—Mr. Shuan done it," he said, with an air of pride.

"What!" I cried, "do you take such savage treatment at his hands?"

"No," said the poor boy, "and so he'll find. See here"; and he showed me a case-knife, which he told me was stolen. "O," said he, "let me see him try; I dare him to; I'll get him sure! O, he ain't the first!"

I have never felt such pity for any one in this wide world as I felt for that half-witted boy; and it began to come over me that the brig *Covenant* was little better than a hell upon the seas.

"Have you no friends?" said I.

He said he had a father in some English seaport. "He was a fine man, too," he said; "but he's dead."

"In Heaven's name," cried I, "can you find no decent life on shore?"

"O no," said he, "they would put me to a trade."

I asked him what trade could be so dreadful as the one he followed, where he was in danger of his life, not alone from wind and sea, but by the cruelty of those who were his masters. He then began to praise the life, and tell what a pleasure it was to get on shore with money in his pocket, and spend it like a man, and buy apples and swagger. "And then it's not all as bad as that," said he; "there's worse off than me: there's the twenty-pounders. And then there's little uns, too. O, littler than me! I tell you, I keep them in order." And so he ran on, and it came to me what he meant by twenty-pounders were those unhappy criminals who were sent overseas to slavery in North America, or the still more unhappy innocents who were kidnapped.

Just then we came to the top of the hill, and looked down on the Ferry. The Firth of Forth narrows at this point to the width of a good-sized river. Right in the middle of the narrows lies an islet with some ruins; on the south shore they have built a pier for the service of the Ferry.

The town of Queensferry lies farther west, and the neighborhood of the inn looked pretty lonely at that time of day, for the boat had just gone north with passengers. A skiff lay beside the pier; this, as Ransome told me, was the brig's boat waiting for the captain; and about half a mile off he pointed out the *Covenant* herself. There was a sea-going bustle on board; and as the wind blew from that quarter, I could hear the song of the sailors as they pulled upon the ropes. I pitied all poor souls that were condemned to sail in the ship.

As soon as we came to the inn, Ransome led us up the stair to a small room. At a table by the chimney, a tall, dark man sat writing. In spite of the heat of the room, he wore a thick sea-jacket, buttoned to the neck, and a tall hairy cap drawn down over his ears.

He got to his feet at once, and offered his large hand to Ebenezer. "I am proud to see you, Mr. Balfour," said he, in a fine deep voice, "and glad that you are here in time. The wind's fair, and the tide upon the turn; we'll see the old coal-bucket burning on the Isle of May before tonight."

It was so warm in the room, away I went back outside, leaving the two men sitting down to a bottle and a great mass of papers; and crossing the road in front of the inn, walked down upon the beach. Little waves beat upon the shore. The smell of sea-water was salt and stirring; the *Covenant* was beginning to shake out her sails; and the spirit of all that I beheld put me in thoughts of far voyages and foreign places.

I returned to the inn and sat down. I asked the landlord if he knew Mr. Rankeillor.

"Ay," said he, "and a very honest man. And, O, by-the-by, was it you that came in with Ebenezer?" And when I had told him yes, "You're no relative of his?" he asked.

I told him no.

"I thought not," said he, "and yet you have a kind of look of Mr. Alexander."

I said it seemed that Ebenezer was ill-seen in the country.

"No doubt," said the landlord. "He's a wicked old man, and there are many would like to see him hanged. And yet he was once a fine young fellow. But that was before the word went around about Mr. Alexander."

"And what was it?"

"Oh, just that he had killed him," said the landlord, "to get the place."

"The Shaws? Is that so? Was my—Was Alexander the eldest son?"

"Indeed was he," said the landlord. "What else would Ebenezer have killed him for?"

And with that he went away.

I sat stunned with the news; my father was the elder brother, and therefore he had been, and now I myself was, the rightful owner of the house and lands that Ebenezer claimed as his own.

The next thing I knew. I heard my uncle calling me, and found him and the captain out on the road before the inn.

"Sir," said the captain, "Mr. Balfour tells me great things of you; and for my part I like your looks. I wish I was longer here, that we might make the better friends; but we'll make the most of what we have. You shall come on board my brig for half an hour, till the ebb sets, and drink a bowl with me."

Now I longed to see the inside of a ship more than words can tell; but I was not going to put myself in danger,

and I told the captain that I had an appointment with the
lawyer.

"Ay, ay," said he, "your uncle passed me word of that.
But, you see, the boat'll set you ashore at the town pier,
and that's but a stone's throw from Rankeillor's house."
And here he suddenly leaned down and whispered in my
ear: "Beware of the old man, he means trouble. Come
aboard till I can get a word with you." And then, passing
his arm through mine, he continued aloud, "But, come,
what can I bring you from the Carolinas? A roll of
tobacco? Indian feather-work? A skin of a wild beast?—
Take your pick."

By this time we were at the boat-side, and he was hand-
ing me in. I did not dream of hanging back; I thought
(poor fool!) that I had found a good friend and helper, and
I was rejoiced to see the ship. As soon as we were all set
in our places, the boat was thrust off from the pier and
began to move over the waters.

As soon as we were alongside the ship, Hoseason, de-
claring that he and I must be the first aboard, ordered a
tackle to be sent down from the main-yard. In this I was
whipped into the air and set down again on the deck,
where the captain stood ready waiting for me, and instantly slipped back his arm under mine.

"But where is my uncle?" said I.

"Ay," said Hoseason, "that's the point."

I felt I was lost. I pulled free of him and ran to the side of the ship. Sure enough, there was the boat pulling for the town, with my uncle sitting in the stern. I gave a piercing cry—"Help, help! Murder!"—and my uncle turned round where he was sitting, and showed me a face full of cruelty.

It was the last thing I saw before strong hands plucked me back from the ship's side; and now a thunderbolt seemed to strike me; I saw a great flash of fire, and fell senseless.

CHAPTER 4
I Go to Sea in the Brig *Covenant*

I CAME TO myself in darkness, in great pain, bound hand and foot. The whole world now heaved up, and now rushed downward; and so sick and hurt was I in body, and my mind so confounded, that it took me a long while to realize that I must be lying somewhere in the belly of the ship.

A small man of about thirty, with green eyes and a tangle of fair hair, came to me by the light of a lantern.

"How goes it?" said he.

I answered by a sob; and my visitor felt my pulse and temples, and set himself to wash and dress the wound upon my head.

"Ay," said he, "a hard hit. But cheer up! The world's not over; you've made a bad start of it, but it'll get better."

The next time he came to see me, I was lying with my eyes wide open in the darkness. I ached in every limb. He was followed by the captain. Neither said a word; but the first set to examining me, and dressed my wound as before, while Hoseason looked me in the face.

"Now, sir, you see for yourself," said the first man: "a high fever, no appetite, no light, no meat: you see for yourself what that means. I want that boy taken out of this hole and put in the forecastle."

"Mr. Riach, I have sailed with ye three cruises," replied the captain. "In all that time, sir, ye should have learned to know me: I'm a hard man; but if ye say the lad will die—"

"Ay, he will!" said Mr. Riach.

"Well, sir, is not that enough?" said Hoseason. "Put him where you please!"

Thereupon the captain went up the ladder; and moments afterwards my bonds were cut, and men came down to carry me up to the quarters under the raised deck, or forecastle, where they laid me in a bunk on some sea blankets. I fell asleep.

It was a blessed thing indeed to open my eyes again upon the daylight, and to find myself with men. The forecastle was a roomy place, set all about with berths, in which the men were seated smoking or lying down asleep. The day being calm and the wind fair, the scuttle—the hole in the ceiling—was open, and not only the good daylight, but from time to time (as the ship rolled) a dusty beam of sunlight shone in, and dazzled and delighted me.

Here I lay for the space of many days, and not only got my health again, but came to know my companions. They were a rough lot indeed, as sailors mostly are. But they had many virtues. They were kind when it occurred to them, simple, and had some glimmerings of honesty. There was one man, of maybe forty, that would sit on my berthside for hours and tell me of his wife and child.

Among other good deeds that they did, they returned my money, which had been shared among them. The ship was bound for the Carolinas; and you must not suppose that I was going to that place merely as an exile. In those days of my youth, white men were still sold into slavery on the plantations, and that was the destiny to which my wicked uncle had condemned me.

The cabin-boy Ransome came in at times from the round-house, where he served, now nursing a bruised leg or arm in silent agony, now raving against the cruelty of Mr. Shuan. It made my heart bleed. I did my best in the small time allowed me to make something like a man, or rather like a boy, of poor Ransome. But he could remember nothing of the time before he came to sea; only that his father had made clocks, and had a bird that could whistle, in the parlor; all else had been blotted out in these years of hardship and cruelty.

Soon the *Covenant* was meeting continual head-winds and tumbling up and down against head-seas, so that the scuttle was almost constantly shut, and the forecastle lighted only by a swinging lantern on a beam. There was constant labor for all hands; but as I was never allowed to set my foot on deck, you can picture to yourselves how weary of my life I grew to be, and how impatient for a change.

One night, about eleven o'clock, a man of Mr. Riach's watch (which was on deck) came below for his jacket; and instantly there began to go a whisper about the forecastle that "Shuan had done for Ransome at last." We had hardly time to get the idea in our heads, far less to speak of it, when the scuttle was flung open, and Captain Hoseason came down the ladder. He looked round the bunks in the tossing light of the lantern; and then, walking straight up to me, said, "My man, we want you to serve in the round-house. You and Ransome are to change berths. Run away aft with you."

Even as he spoke, two seamen appeared in the scuttle, carrying Ransome in their arms; and the ship at that moment giving a great sheer into the sea, and the lantern swinging, the light fell direct on the boy's face. It was as white as wax. The blood in me ran cold, and I drew in my breath as if I had been struck.

"Run away aft; run away aft with ye!" cried Hoseason.

I ran up the ladder on deck. The brig was sheering through a long, cresting swell. The round-house, where I was now to sleep and serve, stood some six feet above the decks. Inside were a fixed table and bench, and two berths, one for the captain and the other for the two mates, turn and turn about. It was all fitted with lockers from top to bottom, so as to stow away the officers' belongings and a part of the ship's stores; all the firearms, except two pieces of brass ordnance, were set in a rack in the aftermost wall of the round-house. The most of the cutlasses were in another place.

A small window with a shutter on each side, and a skylight in the roof, gave it light by day; and after dark there was a lamp always burning. It was burning when I entered, and Mr. Shuan was sitting at the table, with a brandy bottle and tin cup in front of him. He was a tall man, strongly made.

He took no notice of my coming in; nor did he move when the captain followed and leaned on the berth beside me, looking darkly at the mate. Soon Mr. Riach came in. He gave the captain a glance that meant the boy was dead as plain as speaking. We all three stood without a word, staring down at Mr. Shuan, and Mr. Shuan sat without a word, looking hard upon the table.

All of a sudden he put out his hand to take the bottle; and at that Mr. Riach started forward and took it away.

Mr. Shuan was on his feet in a second; he still looked dazed, but he meant murder, ay, and would have done it, for the second time that night, had not the captain stepped in between him and his victim.

"Sit down!" roared the captain. "Ye drunken pig, do ye know what ye've done? Ye've murdered the boy!"

Mr. Shuan seemed to understand; for he sat down again, and put up his hand to his brow.

"Well," he said, "he brought me a dirty cup!"

At that word, the captain and I and Mr. Riach all looked at each other for a second with a frightened look; and then Hoseason walked up to his chief officer, took him by the shoulder, led him across to his bunk, and told him to lie down and go to sleep, as you might speak to a bad child. The murderer cried a little, but he took off his sea-boots and obeyed.

"Ah!" cried Mr. Riach, "ye should have interfered long since. It's too late now."

"Mr. Riach," said the captain, "this night's work must never be known in Dysart. The boy went overboard, sir; that's what the story is; and I would give five pounds out of my pocket it was true!" The pair sat down to drink; and while they did so, the murderer, who had been lying and whimpering in his berth, raised himself upon his elbow and looked at them and at me.

That was the first night of my new duties; and in the course of the next day I had got well into the run of them. I had to serve at meals; all the day through I would be running with a drink to one or other of my three masters; and at night I slept on a blanket thrown on the deck boards at the far end of the round-house.

Though I was clumsy enough and sometimes fell with what I was bringing them, both Mr. Riach and the captain were unusually patient. I believed they were making up with their guilt, and that they would not have been so good with me if they had not been worse with Ransome.

As for Mr. Shuan, the drink, or his crime, had certainly troubled his mind. He never grew used to my being there, stared at me continually (sometimes, I thought, with terror) and more than once drew back from my hand when I was serving him. I was pretty sure from that he had no clear mind of what he had done. On my second day in the round-house, he got up from his seat, and came up close to me.

"You were not here before?" he asked.

"No, sir," said I.

"There was another boy?" he asked again.

"Yes, sir."

"Ah!" said he, "I thought so." He went and sat down, without another word, except to call for brandy.

You may think it strange, but for all the horror I had, I was still sorry for him. He was a married man, with a wife in Leith; but whether or not he had children, I hope not.

Altogether it was no very hard life for the time it lasted, which (as you are to hear) was not long. Mr. Riach, who had been to college, spoke to me like a friend when he was not sulking, and told me many curious things; and even the captain would sometimes unbuckle a bit, and tell me of fine countries he had visited.

Here I was, however, doing dirty work for three men that I looked down upon; that was for the present; and as for the future, I could only see myself slaving in the tobacco fields. As the days came and went, my heart sank lower and lower, till I was even glad of the work which kept me from thinking.

CHAPTER 5
The Man with the Belt of Gold

Mᴏʀᴇ ᴛʜᴀɴ ᴀ week went by, and some days the *Covenant* made a little way; others she was driven actually back. At last we were beaten so far to the south that we tossed and tacked to and fro the whole of the ninth day, within sight of Cape Wrath and the wild, rocky coast on either hand of it. The officers decided to make a fair wind of a foul one and run south.

The tenth afternoon there was a falling swell and a thick, wet, white fog that hid one end of the brig from the other. Maybe about ten at night, I was serving Mr. Riach and the captain at their supper, when the ship struck something with a great sound, and we heard voices singing out. My two masters leaped to their feet, and hurried out.

We had run down a boat in the fog, and she had parted in the middle and gone down to the bottom with all her crew but one. This man had been sitting in the stern as a passenger, while the rest were on the benches rowing. At the moment of the blow, the stern had been thrown into the air, and the man (having his hands free, yet encumbered with an overcoat that came below his knees) had leaped up and caught hold of the brig's bowsprit. It showed he had luck and much agility and unusual strength, that he should have thus saved himself from such a pass.

He was smallish, but well set and as nimble as a goat; his face was sunburnt very dark; his eyes were unusually light; and when he took off his overcoat, he laid a pair of fine silver-mounted pistols on the table, and I saw that he was belted with a great sword. He wore a hat with feathers, a red waistcoat, breeches of black plush, and a blue coat with silver buttons and handsome silver lace.

"I'm vexed, sir, about the boat," said the captain.

"There are some good men gone to the bottom," said the stranger, "that I would rather see on the dry land again than ten boats."

"You've a French soldier's coat upon your back and a Scotch tongue in your head," said the captain.

"So?" said the gentleman in the fine coat. "Well, sir, to be quite plain with you, I am one of those honest gentlemen that were in trouble about the years forty-five and six;* and if I got into the hands of any of the red-coated gentry, it's like it would go hard with me. Now, sir, I was headed for France; and there was a French ship cruising here to pick me up; but she gave us the go-by in the fog—as I wish from the heart that you had done yourself! And the best I can say is this: If you can set me ashore where I was going, I have that upon me will reward you highly for your trouble."

"In France?" said the captain. "No, sir; but where you come from—we might talk of that."

The gentleman took off a money-belt from about his waist, and poured out a guinea or two upon the table, saying, "Thirty guineas on the seaside, or sixty if you set me on the Linnhe Loch. Take it, if you will; if not, you can do your worst."

"Ay," said Hoseason. "And if I give you over to King George's soldiers?"

"You would make a fool's bargain," said the gentleman. "Bring this money within reach of Government, and how much of it'll come to you?"

"Little enough, to be sure," said Hoseason. "Well, what must be must. Sixty guineas, and done. Here's my hand upon it."

---

*The stranger is referring to the Jacobite rebellion of 1745, led by Charles Stuart, the grandson of James II of England. Charles was also known as Bonnie Prince Charlie and the Young Pretender. (His father was known as the Old Pretender.)

"And here's mine."

And then the captain went out, and left me alone in the round-house with the stranger.

"This bottle of yours is dry," he said to me. "It's hard if I'm to pay sixty guineas and be grudged a drink."

"I'll go and ask for the key," said I.

The fog was as thick as ever. The captain and the two officers were out with their heads together. The first word I heard, as I drew softly near, was Mr. Riach's saying, "Couldn't we lure him out of the round-house?"

"Hut!" said Hoseason. "We can get the man in talk inside, and pin him by the two arms."

At this I was seized with fear and anger at these greedy, bloody men that I sailed with.

"Captain," I called out, "the gentleman is seeking a drink, and the bottle's out. Will you give me the key?"

"Why, here's our chance to get the firearms!" Riach cried. And then to me, "Listen, David," he said, "do you know where the pistols are?"

"Ay, ay," put in Hoseason. "David knows; he's a good lad. You see, David my man, that wild Highlandman is a danger to the ship, besides being an enemy to King George.—The trouble is, that all our firearms, great and little, are in the round-house under this man's nose; likewise the powder. Now if I or one of the officers was to go in and take them, he would fall to thinking. But a lad like you might snap up a horn and a pistol or two without remark. And if you can do it cleverly, I'll bear it in mind when it'll be good for you to have friends; and that's when we come to Carolina.—And see here, David, that man has a beltful of gold, and I give you my word that you shall have your fingers in it."

I told him I would do as he wished; and so he gave me the key of the spirit locker, and I began to go slowly back to the round-house. What was I to do? They were dogs

and thieves; they had stolen me from my own country; and was I to hold a candle to a murder? Upon the other hand, what could a boy and a man do against a whole ship's company?

I came into the round-house and saw the man eating his supper under the lamp. I walked right up to the table and put my hand on his shoulder.

"Do you want to be killed?" said I.

He sprang to his feet.

"O!" cried I, "they're all murderers here; it's a ship full of them. They've murdered a boy already. Now it's you."

"Ay, ay," said he; "but they haven't got me yet.—Will you stand by me?"

"That I will!" said I.

"Why, then," said he, "what's your name?"

"David Balfour," said I.

"My name is Stewart. Alan Breck, they call me."

The round-house was built very strong to support the breaching of the seas. Of its five openings, only the skylight and the two doors were large enough for the passage of a man. One door was already closed, but Alan stopped me from closing the other.

"David, that door, being open, is the best part of my defences. You see, I have but one face; but so long as that door is open and my face to it, the best part of my enemies will be in front of me, where I would wish to find them."

Then he gave me from the rack a sword (of which there were a few besides the firearms); and next he set me down to the table with a powder-horn, a bag of bullets and all the pistols, which he asked me to charge.

"How many are against us?" he asked.

I reckoned them up. "Fifteen," said I.

"Well," said he, "that can't be cured. It is my part to keep this door, where I look for the main battle."

"But then, sir," said I, "there is the door behind you, which they may perhaps break in."

"Ay," said he, "and that is a part of your work. No sooner the pistols charged, than you must climb up into that bed where you're close to the window; and if they lift hand against the door, you're to shoot. But that's not all. There's the skylight. And when your face is at the one, you must listen to hear the bursting of the glass of the other."

Scarce had Alan spoken, when the captain showed his face in the open door.

"Stand!" cried Alan, and pointed his sword at him.

"This is a strange return for hospitality!"

"The sooner the clash begins," said Alan, "the sooner you'll taste this steel."

The captain said nothing to Alan, but he looked over at me. "David," said he, "I'll remember this." The next moment he was gone.

"And now," said Alan, "the battle is coming."

Alan drew a knife, which he held in his left hand in case

they should run in under his sword. I clambered up into the berth with an armful of pistols and set open the window where I was to watch. It was a small part of the deck that I could overlook, but enough for our purpose. The sea had gone down, and the wind was steady and kept the sails quiet; so that there was a great stillness in the ship, in which I heard the sound of muttering voices. A little after, and there came a clash of steel upon the deck, by which I knew they were dealing out the cutlasses and one had fallen; and after that, silence again.

All of a sudden, I heard a rush of feet and a roar, then a shout from Alan and a sound of blows. I looked back over my shoulder, and saw Mr. Shuan in the doorway, crossing blades with Alan.

"Look to your window!" said Alan; and as I turned back I saw him pass his sword through the mate's body.

My head was scarce back at the window, before five men, carrying a spare yard for a battering-ram, ran past me to drive the door in. I had never fired a pistol in my life. But it was now or never; and just as they swang the yard, I cried out: "Take that!" and shot into their midst.

I must have hit one of them, for he sang out and gave back a step, and the rest stopped. Before they had time to recover, I sent another ball over their heads; and at my third shot (which went as wide as the second) the whole party threw down the yard and ran for it.

Then I looked round again into the deck-house. The whole place was full of the smoke of my own firing. But there was Alan, standing as before; only now his sword was running blood to the hilt. Right before him on the floor was Mr. Shuan, on his hands and knees, sinking slowly lower; and just as I looked, some of those from behind caught hold of him by the heels and dragged him out.

I told Alan I had winged one, and thought it was the captain.

"And I've settled two," said he. "No, there's not enough blood let; they'll be back again. To your place, David. Unless we can give them a good distaste of us, there'll be no sleep for either you or me."

I settled back to my berth, recharging the three pistols I had fired, and keeping watch with both eye and ear.

There came single call on the sea-pipe, and that was their signal. A knot of them made one rush of it, cutlass in hand, against the door; and at the same moment, the glass in the skylight was dashed in a thousand pieces, and a

man leaped through and landed on the floor. Before he got to his feet, I had clapped a pistol to his back. He had dropped his cutlass as he jumped, and when he felt the pistol, whipped straight round and laid hold of me, roaring out an oath; and at that I gave a shriek and shot him in the midst of his body. He gave the most horrible, ugly groan and fell to the floor. The foot of a second fellow, whose legs were dangling through the skylight, struck me at the same time upon the head; and at that I snatched another pistol and shot him through the thigh, so that he slipped through and tumbled in a lump on his companion's body. I clapped the muzzle to him and fired.

I heard Alan shout as if for help. He had kept the door for so long; but one of the seamen, while he was engaged with the others, had run in under his guard and caught him about the body. Alan was knifing him with his left hand, but the fellow clung like a leech. Another had broken in and had his cutlass raised. The door was filled with their faces. I thought we were lost, and catching up my cutlass, came at them.

But I had not time to be of help. The wrestler dropped at last; and Alan, leaping back to get his distance, ran upon the others like a bull, roaring as he went. They broke before him like water, turning, and running, and falling one against another in their haste. The sword in his hands flashed like lightning; and at every flash there came the scream of a man hurt. I was still thinking we were lost, when lo! they were all gone.

The round-house was like a shambles; three were dead inside, another lay in agony across the threshold; and there were Alan and I victorious and unhurt.

He came up to me with open arms, and embraced me. "David," said he, "I love you like a brother. And O, man," he cried happily, "am I not a wonderful fighter?"

Then he turned to the four enemies, passed his sword clean through each of them, and tumbled them out of doors one after the other. As he did so, he kept humming and singing and whistling to himself, like a man trying to recall a tune; only what *he* was trying was to make one. Soon he sat down upon the table, sword in hand; the tune that he was making all the time began to run a little clearer; and then out he burst with a great voice into a Gaelic song.

In the meanwhile, the battle was no sooner over than I was glad to stagger to a seat. There was a tightness in my chest; the thought of the two men I had shot sat upon me like a nightmare; and all of a sudden, I began to sob and cry like any child.

Alan clapped my shoulder, and said I was a brave lad and needed nothing but a sleep.

"I'll take the first watch," said he. "You've done well by me, David."

So I made up my bed on the floor; and he took the first spell, pistol in hand and sword on knee, three hours by the captain's watch upon the wall. Then he roused me up, and I took my turn of three hours; before the end of which it was broad day, and a very quiet morning. At last, looking out of the door of the round-house, I saw the great stone hills of Skye on the right hand, and, a little more astern, the strange Isle of Rum.

Alan and I sat down to breakfast about six. The floor was covered with broken glass and blood.

"Depend upon it," said Alan, "we shall hear more of them before long."

He took a knife from the table, and cut me off one of the silver buttons from his coat. "I had them," he said, "from my father, Duncan Stewart; and now give you one of them to be a keepsake for last night's work. And wherever you go and show that button, the friends of Alan Breck will come around you."

We were hailed by Mr. Riach from the deck, asking for a talk. I climbed through the skylight and sat on the edge of it, pistol in hand.

"This is a bad job," said he.

"It was none of our choosing," said I.

"The captain would like to speak to your friend.—What we want is to be quits with him."

I consulted with Alan, and a meeting was agreed to.

The captain came and said to Alan, "You've made a sore hash of my brig; I haven't hands enough left to sail her. There is nothing left me, sir, but to put back into the port

of Glasgow after more sailors."

"No," said Alan, "that'll not do. You'll just have to set me ashore as we agreed."

"Ay," said Hoseason, "but my first officer is dead. There's none of the rest of us acquainted with this coast, sir; and it's one very dangerous to ships."

"Set me on dry ground, within thirty miles of my own country; except in the country of the Campbells," said Alan, "and you'll have sixty guineas."

CHAPTER 6
I Hear of the "Red Fox"

BEFORE WE HAD done cleaning out the round-house, a breeze sprang up. This blew off the rain and brought out the sun.

And here I must explain; and the reader would do well to look at a map. On the day when the fog fell and we ran down Alan's boat, we had been running through Little Minch. At dawn after the battle, we lay becalmed to the east of the Isle of Canna. Now to get from there to the Linnhe Loch, the straight course was through the Sound of Mull. But the captain had no chart; he was afraid to sail his brig so deep among the islands; and he preferred to go by west of Tiree and come up under the southern coast of the Isle of Mull.

By nightfall, we had turned the end of Tiree. Meanwhile, the early part of the day was very pleasant; sailing, as we were, in a bright sunshine and with many mountainous islands upon different sides. Alan and I sat in the round-house with the doors open on each side, and smoked a pipe or two of the captain's tobacco. It was at this time we heard each other's stories, and I gained some knowledge of that wild Highland country on which I was so soon to land.

I went first, telling him all my misfortune. But when I came to mention that good friend of mine, Mr. Campbell the minister, Alan cried out that he hated all that were of that name.

"Why," said I, "he is a man you should be proud to give your hand to."

"I know nothing I would help a Campbell to," said he, "unless it was a bullet. If I lay dying, I would crawl upon my knees to the window for a shot at one."

"Why, Alan," I cried, "what do you have against the Campbells?"

"Well," said he, "you know that I am an Appin Stewart, and the Campbells have long bothered and destroyed those of my name; ay, and stolen lands from us by treachery— but never with the sword! They used lying words, lying papers, and the show of it being legal, to make a man the more angry."

"You that are so wasteful of your buttons," said I, "I can hardly think you would be a good judge of business."

"Ah!" said he, smiling, "I got my wastefulness from the same man I got the buttons from; and that was my poor father, Duncan Stewart! He was the prettiest man of his kindred; and the best swordsman in the Highlands, David, and that is the same as to say, in all the world."

"I think he was not the man to leave you rich."

"And that's true," said Alan. "He left me my trousers to cover me, and little else besides. And that was how I came to enlist, which would be a hard lot for me if I fell among the red-coats."

"What," cried I, "were you in the English army?"

"That was I," said Alan. "But I deserted to the right side—and that's some comfort."

"Dear, dear. The punishment for desertion is death."

"Ay," said he, "if they got their hands on me."

I asked him, "You are a man of the French king's—what

tempts you back into this country?"

"Tut!" said Alan. "I have been back every year since forty-six!"

"And what brings you, man?"

"Well, you see, I weary for my friends and country," said he. "France is a fine place, no doubt; but I weary for the heather and the deer. But the heart of the matter is the business of my chief, Ardshiel, captain of the clan. Now the tenants of Appin have to pay a rent to King George; but their hearts are loyal, and what with love and a bit of pressure, and maybe a threat or two, the poor folk scrape up a second rent for Ardshiel. Well, David, I'm the hand that carries it back to France for him." And he struck the belt around his body, so that the guineas rang.

"I call it noble of those folk," I cried. "I'm loyal to King George, but I call it noble."

"Ay," said he, "you're a Whig, but you're a gentleman. Now if you were one of the cursed Campbells, or if you were the Red Fox . . . "

"And who is the Red Fox?"

"When the men of the clans were defeated at Culloden, and the good cause lost, Ardshiel had to flee like a poor deer upon the mountains—he and his lady and his children. A sad time of it we had before we got him shipped; and while he still lay in the heather, the English rogues, that could not kill him, were striking at his rights. They stripped him of his powers; they stripped him of his lands; they plucked the weapons from the hands of his clansmen; ay, and the very clothes off their backs—so that it's now a sin to wear a tartan plaid, and a man may be cast into prison if he has a kilt about his legs. One thing they couldn't kill. That was the love the clansmen had for their chief. These guineas are the proof of it. And now, in there steps a man, a Campbell, red-headed Colin of Glenure! In he steps, and gets papers from King George, to be King's agent on the lands of Appin. By-and-by, it came to his ears how the poor folk of Appin were wringing their very plaids to get a second rent, and send it over-seas for Ardshiel and his poor children. Well, the black Campbell blood in him ran wild. What! should a Stewart get a bite of bread, and him not be able to prevent it? No. Ardshiel was to starve: that was the thing he aimed at. And he would drive them that fed him out. Therefore he sent for lawyers, and papers, and red-coats to stand at his back. And the kindly folk of that country must all pack and tramp, every father's son out of his father's house, and out of the place where he was bred and fed!"

There was so much anger in Alan's voice that I thought it wise to change the conversation. I expressed my wonder how, with the Highlands covered with troops, a man in Alan's situation could come and go without arrest.

"It's easier than ye would think," he said. "A hillside is like one road; if there's a sentry at one place, ye just go by another. And then the heather's a great help. And everywhere there are friends' houses and friends' barns and haystacks. And besides, when folk talk of a country covered with troops, it's not truly so. A soldier covers no more of it than his boot-soles. I have fished a water with a sentry on the other side of the brook, and killed a fine trout; and I have sat in a heather bush within six feet of another, and learned a real bonny tune from his whistling. This was it," said he, and whistled me the air.

"And then, besides," he continued, "it's not so bad now as it was in forty-six. The Highlands are what they call pacified. But not for long, with men like Ardshiel in exile and men like the Red Fox harassing the poor at home. But it's not easy to know what folk'll bear, and what they will not. Or why would Red Colin be riding his horse all over my poor country of Appin, and never a fine lad to put a bullet in him?"

And with this Alan fell into a long silent thought.

It was already late at night, when Hoseason clapped his hand into the round-house door.

"Here," said he, "come out and see if you can pilot.—My brig's in danger!"

Alan and I stepped on deck.

The sky was clear; it blew hard, and was bitter cold; the moon shone brightly. Away on the lee bow, a thing like a fountain rose out of the moonlit sea, and immediately after we heard a low sound of roaring.

"What do you call that?" asked the captain.

"The sea breaking on a reef," said Alan.

"If it was only one," said Hoseason.

And sure enough, just as he spoke there came a second fountain farther to the south.

"There!" said Hoseason. "You see for yourself. If I had known of these reefs, or if Shuan had lived, it's not sixty guineas, no, nor six hundred, would have made me risk my brig in such a stoneyard!"

"It sticks in my mind there are ten miles of the Torran Rocks," said Alan.

"There's a way through them, I suppose?" said the captain.

"Doubtless," said Alan. "It somehow runs in my mind that it is a clearer near the land."

"Well," said the captain, "we're in for it now, and may as well crack on."

With that he gave an order to the steersman, and sent Riach to the foretop. There were only five men on deck, counting the officers.

"The sea to the south is thick," Riach cried; and then, after a while, "it does seem clearer in by the land."

"Well, sir," said Hoseason to Alan, "we'll try your way of

it. Pray God you're right."

As we got nearer to the turn of the land at the end of the Isle of Mull, the reefs began to appear here and there on our very path; and Mr. Riach sometimes cried down to us to change the course. Sometimes, indeed, none too soon; for one reef was so close that when a sea burst upon it the spray fell upon the deck and wetted us like rain.

"Goodness, David," said Alan, "this is not the kind of death I fancy!"

"What, Alan!" I cried, "you're not afraid?"

"No," said he, wetting his lips, "but you'll allow it's a cold ending."

By this time, now and then sheering to one side or the other to avoid a reef, but still hugging the wind and the land, we got round Iona and began to come alongside Mull. The tide at the tail of the land ran very strong, and threw the brig about.

"Keep her away a point," sang out Mr. Riach. "Reef to windward!"

And just at that time the tide caught the brig, and threw the wind out of her sails. She came round into the wind like a top, and the next moment struck the reef with such a crash as threw us all flat upon the deck, and came near to shake Mr. Riach from his place upon the mast.

I was on my feet in a minute. The reef on which we had struck was close in under the southwest end of Mull, off a little isle they call Earraid, which lay low and black upon the larboard. Sometimes a swell broke clean over us; sometimes it only ground the poor brig upon the reef, so that we could hear her beat herself to pieces; and as well there was the great noise of the sails, and the singing of the wind, and the flying of the spray in the moonlight, and the sense of danger.

I observed Mr. Riach and the seamen busy round the skiff, and ran over to assist them. All the time of our work-

ing to clear the boat, I asked Alan, looking across at the
shore, what country it was; and he answered, it was the
worst possible for him, for it was a land of the Campbells.

Well, we had the boat about ready to be launched, when
one of the wounded men, keeping a watch on the seas,
cried out, "For God's sake, hold on!"

There followed a sea so huge that it lifted the brig right
up and turned her over on her beam. At the sudden tilting
of the ship I was cast clean over the side into the sea.

I went down and drank my fill, and then came up, and
got a blink of the moon, and then down again. I was being
hurled along, and beaten upon and choked, and then swal-
lowed whole. Soon I found I was holding to a spar, which
helped me somewhat. And then all of a sudden I was in
quiet water, and began to come to myself.

It was the spare yard I had got hold of, and I was amazed to see how far I had travelled from the brig. I hailed her, indeed; but it was plain she was already out of cry. She was still holding together; but whether or not they had yet launched the boat, I was too far off and too low down to see.

I now lay quite becalmed, and began to feel that a man can die of cold as well as of drowning. The shores of Earraid were close in. I had no skill in swimming, but when I laid hold upon the yard with both arms, and kicked out with both feet, I soon began to find that I was moving. After an hour of kicking and splashing, I had got well into a sandy bay surrounded by low hills. I thought in my heart I had never seen a place so deserted and desolate. But it was dry land.

CHAPTER 7
The Islet

WITH MY STEPPING ashore I began the most unhappy part of my adventures. I climbed a hill, and when I got to the top the dawn was come. There was no sign of the brig, which must have lifted from the reef and sunk. The boat, too, was nowhere to be seen.

I was afraid to think what had befallen my shipmates. I set off eastward, along the south coast, hoping to find a house where I might warm myself, and perhaps get news of those I had lost. After a little while my way was stopped by a creek or inlet of the sea, which seemed to run pretty deep into the land; and as I had no means to get across, I must needs change my direction to go about the end of it. It was the roughest kind of walking, nothing but a jumble of granite rocks with heather in among. At last I came to a rise, and it burst upon me that I was cast upon a little barren isle, and cut off on every side by the salt seas.

Instead of the sun rising to dry me, it came on to rain. It occurred to me that perhaps the creek was fordable. But not three yards from shore, I plumped in head over ears.

The time I spent upon the island, which I later learned was Earraid, is still so horrible a thought to me, that I must pass it lightly over. In all the books I have read of people cast away, they had either their pockets full of tools, or a chest of things would be thrown upon the beach along with them. My case was very different. I had nothing in my pockets but money and Alan's silver button.

The second day I crossed the island to all sides. There was no one part of it better than another; it was all desolate and rocky; nothing living on it but birds which I lacked the means to kill.

Now, from a little up a hillside over a bay, I could catch a sight of a great, ancient church and the roofs of the people's houses in Iona. Over the low country of the Ross, I saw smoke go up, morning and evening. This sight I had of men's homes and comfortable lives kept hope alive, and helped me eat my raw shell-fish.

The second day passed, but on the third in the morning I saw a red-deer standing in the rain on the top of the island. I supposed he must have swum the strait; though what should bring any creature to Earraid, was more than I could fancy. My clothes were beginning to rot; my stockings in particular were quite worn through. And yet the worst was not yet come.

All of a sudden, a fishing boat with a brown sail and a pair of fishermen aboard of it, came flying round a corner of the isle, bound for Iona. I shouted out, and then fell on my knees on the rock and reached up my hands and prayed to them. They were near enough to hear—I could even see the color of their hair; they cried out in Gaelic, and laughed. But the boat never turned aside, and flew on, right before my eyes, for Iona.

I ran along the shore from rock to rock, crying after them.

The next day I found my strength very low. But the sun shone, the air was sweet, and what I managed to eat of the shell-fish agreed well with me and revived my courage.

I was scarce back on the highest rock on Earraid (where I went always the first thing after I had eaten) before I observed a boat. I began at once to hope and fear. She was coming straight to Earraid!

I ran to the seaside and out, from one rock to another, as far as I could go. It was the same boat and the same two men as yesterday, but now there was a third man along with them.

As soon as they were come within easy speech, they let down their sail and lay quiet. The new man tee-hee'd with laughter as he talked and looked at me.

Then he stood up in the boat and addressed me a long while, speaking fast and with many wavings of his hand. I picked out a word, "tide." Then I had a flash of hope. I remembered he was always waving his hand towards the mainland of the Ross.

"Do you mean when the tide is out—?" I cried.

"Yes, yes," said he. "Tide."

At that I turned tail, leaped back the way I had come, from one stone to another, and set off running across the isle. In about half an hour I came out upon the shores of the creek; and, sure enough, it was shrunk into a little trickle of water, through which I dashed, not above my knees, and landed with a shout on the main island.

A sea-bred boy would not have stayed a day on Earraid; which is only what they call a tidal islet, and can be entered and left twice in every twenty-four hours. I had starved with cold and hunger on that island for close upon one hundred hours. But for the fishermen, I might have left my bones there.

The Ross of Mull, which I had now got upon, was rugged and trackless, like the isle I had just left. I aimed as well as I could for the smoke I had seen so often from the island, and came upon a house in the bottom of a little hollow about five or six at night. In front of it, an old gentleman sat smoking his pipe in the sun.

With what little English he had, he gave me to understand that my shipmates had got safe ashore, and had eaten in that very house on the day after. He said that I must be the lad with the silver button.

"Why, yes!"

"Well, then," said the old gentleman, "I have a word for you, that you are to follow your friend to his country, by Torosay." He and his good wife fed me, and let me sleep till the next day.

I set out and wandered, meeting plenty of people and, along the roads, many beggars. At night I paid for lodgings in lonely houses.

On my fourth day of travel, I overtook a great, ragged man, moving pretty fast but feeling before him with a staff. He was quite blind, and as we began to go along together, I saw the steel butt of a pistol sticking from under the flap of his coat-pocket. I could not see what a blind man could be doing with a pistol.

He told me he would guide me to Torosay for a drink of brandy.

I said I did not see how a blind man could be a guide; but at that he laughed aloud, and said his stick was eyes enough for an eagle.

"In the Isle of Mull, at least," said he, "where I know every stone and heather-bush. See, now," he said, striking right and left, "down there a creek is running; and at the head of it there stands a bit of a small hill with a stone cocked upon the top of that; and it's hard at the foot of the hill, that the way runs by to Torosay; and the way here is plainly trodden, and will show grassy through the heather."

I had to own he was right in every feature, and told my wonder.

He then began to question me, where I came from, whether I was rich, whether I could change a five-shilling piece for him, and all the time he kept edging up to me and I avoiding him. We were now upon a sort of green cattle-track which crossed the hills towards Torosay, and we kept changing sides upon that like dancers. I took a pleasure in this game of blindman's bluff; but he grew angrier and angrier, and at last began to swear in Gaelic and to strike for my legs with his staff.

Then I told him that, sure enough, I had a pistol in my pocket as well as he, and if he did not strike across the hill due south I would even blow his brains out.

He became at once very polite, and after trying to soften me for some time, but quite in vain, he cursed me once more and took himself off.

At Torosay, on the Sound of Mull and looking over to the mainland of Morven, there was an inn, where I stayed the night, having travelled the greater part of that big and crooked Island of Mull, from Earraid to Torosay, fifty miles as the crow flies, and (with my wanderings) much nearer a hundred, in four days.

CHAPTER 8
The Death of the Red Fox

THERE IS A regular ferry from Torosay to Kinlochaline on the mainland. The passage was a very slow affair. The skipper of the boat was Neil Roy Macrob; and since Macrob was one of the names of Alan's clansmen, and Alan himself had sent me to that ferry, I was eager to speak with him. At Kinlochaline, I did so.

He gave me my route. This was to lie the night in Kinlochaline in the public inn; to cross Morven the next day to Ardgour, and lie the night in the house of one John of the Claymore, who was warned that I might come; the third day, to be set across one loch at Corran and another at Balachulish, and then ask my way to the house of James of the Glens, at Aucharn in Duror of Appin. There was a good deal of ferrying, as you hear; the sea in all this part running deep into the mountains and winding about their roots. It makes the country strong to hold and difficult to travel, but full of startling sights.

I had some other advice from Neil: to speak with no one by the way, to avoid Whigs, Campbells, and the red-soldiers; to leave the road and lie in the bush if I saw any of the latter coming, "for it was never good to meet them"; and in brief, to conduct myself like a robber or a French spy, as perhaps Neil thought me.

On the last leg of that journey, into Appin, I set out with a fisherman across the Linnhe Loch. The mountains on either side were high, rough and barren. It seemed a hard country for people to care as much about as Alan did.

I was let off near the wood of birches, growing on a steep, craggy side of a mountain that overhung the loch. I sat down to eat some oat-bread and think about my situation. What I ought to do, why I was going to join myself with an outlaw like Alan, whether I should not be acting more like a man of sense to tramp back to the south country direct; these were the doubts that now began to come in on me.

As I was so sitting and thinking, a sound of men and horses came to me through the wood; and soon after, at a turning in the road, I saw four travellers come into view. The first was a great, red-headed gentleman, who carried his hat in his hand and fanned himself. The second, by his black garb and white wig, I took to be a lawyer. The third was a servant. The fourth, who brought up the tail, I had seen his like before and knew him to be a sheriff's officer. When the first came alongside of me, I rose up and asked him the way to Aucharn.

"And what do you seek in Aucharn?" said Colin Roy Campbell of Glenure, him they called the Red Fox; for he it was that I had stopped.

"The man that lives there," said I.

"Why does this honest man so far from his country come seeking the brother of Ardshiel?" As he said this he turned to look at the lawyer.

But just as he turned there came the shot of a firelock from higher up the hill; and with the very sound of it the Red Fox fell upon the road.

"O, I am dead!" he cried. With that he gave a great sigh, and passed away.

I stood staring in a kind of horror. The sheriff's officer had run back at the first sound of the shot, to hasten the coming of the soldiers. To help them I began to scramble away up the hill, crying out, "The murderer! the murderer!"

When I got to the top of the first steepness, and could

see some part of the open mountain, the murderer was moving away at no great distance. He was a big man, in a black coat, with metal buttons, and carried a long gun.

"Here!" I cried. "I see him!"

At that the murderer gave a little, quick look over his shoulder, and began to run. The next moment he was lost in a fringe of birches; then he came out again on the upper side, where I could see him climbing like a monkey, and then I saw him no more.

All this time I had been running, and had got a good way up, when a voice cried upon me to stop. I was at the edge of the upper wood, and so now when I halted and looked back, I saw all the open part of the hill below me.

The lawyer and the sheriff's officer were standing just

above the road, crying and waving to me to come back; and on their left, the red-coats, muskets in hand, were beginning to struggle out of the lower wood.

"Why should I come back?" I cried. "Come on!"

"Ten pounds if you take that lad!" cried the lawyer. "He's an accomplice. He was posted here to hold us in talk."

At that word (which I could hear quite plainly, though it was to the soldiers and not to me that he was crying it) my heart came in my mouth with a new kind of terror.

The soldiers began to spread, some of them to run.

"Duck in here among the trees," said a voice close by.

I obeyed; and as I did so, I heard the firelocks bang and the balls whistle in the birches.

Just inside the shelter of the trees I found Alan Breck standing, with a fishing-rod. He said, "Come!" and set off running along the side of the mountain towards Balachulish.

Now we ran among the birches; now stooping behind low humps upon the mountainside; now crawling on all fours among the heather. I had neither time to think nor speak. Every now and then Alan would straighten himself to his full height and look back; and every time he did so, there came a far-away cheering and crying of the soldiers.

At last we came to the upper wood of Lettermore, where we lay down panting like dogs.

"Well," he said finally, "that was a hot one, David."

I said nothing. I had seen murder done, and a great red-faced, jovial gentleman struck out of life in a moment. Here was murder done upon the man Alan hated; here was Alan hiding in the trees and running from the troops; and whether his was the hand that fired or only the head that ordered, meant little. My only friend in that wild country was guilty in the first degree; I could not look upon his face; I would have rather been alone in the rain on my cold isle, than in the warm wood beside a murderer.

"Are you still tired?" he asked.

"No," I said. "But you and I must part. I liked you very well, Alan, but your ways are not mine, and not God's."

"I will hardly part from you, David, without some kind of reason," said Alan.

"You know very well that the Red Fox lies in his blood upon the road. Do you mean to say you had no hand in it?"

"I will tell you, Davie, as one friend to another, if I were going to kill a gentleman, it would not be in my own country, to bring trouble to my clan; and I would not go without a sword and gun, with a fishing-rod upon my back."

"Well," said I, "that's true."

"I swear I had no part in it."

"I thank God for that!" cried I, and offered him my hand. He did not appear to see it. "But what a fuss you make about a Campbell," said he. "There are such a lot of them."

"But do you know who did it?" I asked. "Do you know that man in the black coat?"

"I have no clear mind about his coat," said Alan; "but it sticks in my head that it was blue."

"Blue or black, did ye know him?" said I.

"I couldn't swear to him," said Alan. "He went very close by me, to be sure, but it's a strange thing that I should just have been tying my shoes."

"Can you swear that you don't know him, Alan?"

"Not yet," said he; "but I've a grand memory for forgetting."

"Yet you exposed yourself and me to draw the soldiers away from him," I said.

"So would any gentleman," said Alan. "You and me were innocent of that event."

"The better reason, since we were falsely suspected, that we should get clear," I cried. "The innocent should surely come before the guilty."

"Why, David," said he, "the innocent have a chance in

court; but for the lad that shot the bullet, I think the best place for him will be the heather."

He then said we had not much time, but must both flee that country; he, because he was a wanted man, and the whole of Appin would now be searched, and I, because they would think I was certainly involved in the murder.

I asked him where we should flee; and as he told me "to the Lowlands," I was a little better inclined to go with him; for, indeed, I was growing impatient to get back and have the upper-hand of my uncle.

"I'll chance it, Alan," said I. "I'll go with you."

"But mind you," he said, "it's no small thing. Your life shall be like the hunted deer's, and you shall sleep with your hand upon your weapons. But if you ask what other chance you have, I answer: None. Either take to the heather with me, or else hang by their justice."

"And that's a choice very easily made," said I; and we shook hands upon it.

On the way to Aucharn, each of us narrated his adventures; and I shall here set down so much of Alan's as seems either curious or needful.

It appears he ran to the side of the ship as soon as the wave was passed; saw me, and lost me, and saw me again, as I tumbled in the roost; and at last had one glimpse of me clinging on the yard. It was this that put him in some hope I would maybe get to land after all, and made him leave those clues and messages which had brought me to that unlucky country of Appin.

In the meanwhile, those still on the brig had got the skiff launched, and one or two were on board of her already, when there came a second wave greater than the first, and heaved the brig out of her place, catching it on the reef. Water began to pour into her. All who were on deck tumbled one after another into the skiff and fell to their oars. They were not two hundred yards away, when there came a third great sea; and at that the brig lifted clean over the reef; her canvas filled for a moment, and she seemed to sail in chase of them, but settling all the while; and soon she drew down and down, as if a hand was drawing her; and the sea closed over the *Covenant.*

They had scarce set foot upon the beach when Hoseason told his men to lay hands upon Alan, saying that he had a lot of gold, that he had been the cause of losing the brig and drowning all their comrades. It was seven against one; and in that part of the shore there was no rock that Alan could set his back to; and the sailors began to spread out and come behind him.

"And then," said Alan, "Riach took up my defense, and argued against their attack. Then he cried to me to run, and indeed I thought it good advice, and ran. The last I saw they were all in a knot upon the beach, and the fists were going. So I set my best foot forward and got through the strip of Campbells in that end of Mull."

CHAPTER 9
The Flight in the Heather

NIGHT FELL as we were walking, and the clouds thickened, so that it felt extremely dark. The way we went was over rough mountainsides. At last, we came to the top of the valley, and saw lights below us. Alan whistled three times; having thus set the folks' minds at rest, we came down the valley, and were met at the yard gate by a tall man of more than fifty, who cried out to Alan:

"There has been a dreadful accident. It will bring trouble on the country."

"Hoots!" said Alan, "ye must take the sour with the sweet, James. Colin Roy is dead, and be thankful for that!"

"Ay," said James, "but now that it's done, Alan, who's to

bear the blame of it? The accident fell out in Appin—it's Appin must pay; and I am a man that has a family."

While he and Alan conversed, I looked about me at the servants. Some were on ladders, digging in the thatch of the house or the farm buildings, from which they brought out guns, swords, and different weapons of war; others carried them away; and by the sound of it farther down the valley, they were burying them.

"We're just setting the house in order, Alan," explained James. "They'll search Appin, and we must dig the guns and swords into the moss, ye see. And these French clothes you're wearing, we'll bury them, too."

"No, you won't!" cried Alan. He went off into the barn, and James took me into the house, and one of his sons gave me a change of clothing of which I had stood so long in need, and a pair of Highland shoes made of deer-leather, rather strange at first, but after a little practice very easy to the feet.

After Alan had told his story, it was understood that I was to escape with him, and they were all busy with our equipment. They gave us each a sword and pistols; and with these, some powder and bullets, a bag of oatmeal, an iron pan, and a bottle of brandy. Money, indeed, was lacking. I had about two guineas left, the rest having been lost in the sea off the islet; Alan's belt having been lost as well.

"This'll not do," said Alan.

"Ye must find a safe bit somewhere near by," said James, "and get word to me."

"Hoot, hoot," said Alan. "Tomorrow there'll be a fine to-do in Appin, a fine riding of soldier red-coats; and it would be well, Davie, for you and me to be gone."

We said farewell to James's family, and set out again, in a fine, mild night, and over much the same broken country as before.

Sometimes we walked, sometimes we ran; and as it drew

on to morning, walked ever the less and ran the more. Though that country appeared to be deserted, there were huts and houses of people, of which we must have passed more than twenty, hidden in quiet places of the hills. When we came to one of these, Alan would leave me, and go himself and rap upon the side of the house and speak a while at the window, passing the news of the murder.

For all our hurry, day began to come in while we were still far from any shelter. We were in a large valley, full of rocks and where ran a foaming river. Wild mountains stood around it; there grew neither grass nor trees.

"This is no place for you and me," said Alan. "This is a place they're bound to watch."

And with that he ran down to the waterside, in a part where the river was split in two among three rocks. Alan jumped clean upon the middle rock and fell there on his

hands and knees to check himself, for that rock was small and he might have pitched over on the far side. I had scarce time to measure the distance before I followed him, and he had caught and stopped me.

So there we stood, side by side upon a small rock slippery with spray, a far broader leap in front of us, and the river crashing upon all sides. When I saw where I was, I put my hand over my eyes. Alan took me and shook me; I saw he was speaking, but the roaring of the falls prevented me from hearing. Then, putting his hands to his mouth, and his mouth to my ear, he shouted, "Hang or drown!" and turning his back upon me, leaped over the farther branch of the stream, and landed safe.

I was now alone upon the rock, which gave me the more room. I bent low on my knees and flung myself forth. Sure enough, it was but my hands that reached the full length; these slipped, and I was sliddering back into the river, when Alan seized me, first by the hair, then by the collar, and with a great strain dragged me into safety.

Never a word he said, but set off running again for his life, and I must stagger to my feet and run after him. I kept stumbling as I ran; and when at last Alan paused under a great rock that stood there among a number of others, it was none too soon.

By rights it was two rocks leaning together at the top, both twenty feet high. Even Alan failed twice in an attempt to climb them; and it was only at the third trial, and then by standing on my shoulders and leaping up with such force as I thought must have broken my collar bone, that he secured a place. Once there, he let down his leather belt; and with that and the shallow footholds in the rock, I scrambled up beside him.

Then I saw why we had come there; for the two rocks, being both somewhat hollow on the top and sloping one to the other, made a kind of dish or saucer, where as many as three or four men might have lain hidden. The dawn had come clear; we could see the stony sides of the valley.

"Go you to your sleep, lad, and I'll watch," said Alan.

I lay down to sleep; the last thing I heard was the crying of eagles.

I was roughly awakened, and found Alan's hand pressed upon my mouth.

"Wheesht!" he whispered. "Ye were snoring." He peered over the edge of the rock, and signed to me to do the like.

It was now high day, cloudless, and very hot. About half a mile up the water was a camp of red-coats; a big fire blazed in their midst, at which some were cooking; and near by, on the top of a rock about as high as ours, there stood a sentry, with the sun sparkling on his arms. All the way down along the riverside were posted other sentries; but as the stream suddenly swelled by the water from a large brook, they were more widely set.

I took but one look at them, and ducked again.

"Ye, see," said Alan, "this was what I was afraid of, Davie: that they would watch the valley. They began to come in about two hours ago, and, man! but ye're a grand hand at sleeping! We're in a tight spot. If they get up the sides of the hill, they could easy spy us with a glass. Come night we'll try at getting by the posts down the water."

"And what are we to do till night?" I asked.

"Lie here," said he, "and toast."

The rock grew so heated, a man could scarce endure the touch of it; and the little patch between the two rocks of earth and fern, which kept cooler, was only large enough for one at a time. We took turn about to lie on the naked rock. All the while we had no water, only raw brandy, which was worse than nothing.

The boredom and pain of these hours upon the rock grew only the greater as day went on; the rock getting still the hotter and the sun fiercer.

At last, about two, there came a patch of shade on the east side of our rock, which was the side sheltered from the soldiers.

"As well one death as another," said Alan, and slipped over the edge and dropped on the ground on the shadowy side.

I followed him at once. Here, then, we lay for an hour or two, aching from head to foot, as weak as water, lying quite exposed to any soldier who should have strolled that way. None came, however, all passing by on the other side; so that our rock continued to be our shield.

Soon we began to get a little strength; and as the soldiers were now lying closer along the riverside, Alan proposed that we should try a start. We began to slip from rock to rock, one after the other, now crawling flat on our bellies in the shade, now making a run for it.

By sundown we had made some distance, even by our slow rate of progress, though the sentry on the rock was still plainly in our view. But now we came on a deep, rushing brook. We cast ourselves on the ground and plunged head and shoulders in the water.

We lay there (the banks hid us), drank again and again, and at last, being wonderfully renewed, we got out the meal-bag and made drammach in the iron pan. This, though it is but cold water mingled with oatmeal, yet makes a good enough dish for a hungry man.

As soon as the shadow of the night had fallen, we set forth again. The way was very tricky, lying up the steep sides of mountains and along the brows of cliffs.

Finally Alan judged us out of ear-shot of all our enemies; throughout the rest of our night-march he whistled many tunes on the great, dark, deserted mountain.

It was still dark when we reached our destination, a cleft in the head of the great mountain, with a stream running through the midst, and upon the one hand a shallow cave in a rock. The stream was full of trout; the wood of doves. From the mouth of the cleft we looked down upon a part of Mamore, and on the sea-loch that divides that country from Appin. The name of the cleft was the Heugh of Corrynakiegh; and although it was often covered with clouds, yet it was on the whole a pleasant place, and the five days we lived in it went happily.

We slept in the cave, making our bed of heather bushes, and covering ourselves with Alan's overcoat. There was a low concealed place, in the turning of the glen, where we were so bold as to make fire: so that we could warm ourselves when the clouds set in, and cook hot porridge, and grill the little trouts that we caught with our hands.

In the meanwhile, you are not to suppose that we forgot our chief business, which was to get away.

"It will be many a long day," Alan said to me on our first morning, "before the red-coats think upon seeking us here; so now we must get word sent to James, and he must find the silver for us."

"And how shall we send that word?" said I. "We are here in a deserted place, which we dare not leave."

"Ay?" said Alan. "Ye're a man of small imaginings, David."

Getting a piece of wood, he made it in a cross, the four ends of which he blackened on the coals. Then he asked, "Could ye lend me my button?"

I gave him the button; he strung it on a strip of his

overcoat which he had used to bind the cross; and tying in a little sprig of birch and another of fir, he said, "Now, there is a little hamlet not very far from Corrynakiegh. Many friends of mine are living there whom I could trust with my life, and some that I am not just so sure of. Ye see, David, there will be money upon our heads. So, I would rather they didn't see me. When it comes dark again, I will steal down into that hamlet, and set this that I have been making in the window of a good friend, John Breck Maccoll."

"If he finds it, what is he to think?"

"I am afraid he will think little enough of it! But this is what I have in mind. This cross is something like a fiery cross, which is the signal of gathering in our clans. Yet he will know the clan is not to rise, for there it is standing in his window, and he'd heard no word with it. Then he will see my button, and that was Duncan Stewart's. And then he will say to himself, 'The son of Duncan is in the heather, and has need of me.' "

"Well," said I, "it may be. But even supposing so, there is a good deal of heather between here and the Forth."

"But then John will see the sprig of birch and the sprig of pine; and he will say to himself, 'Alan will be lying in a wood which is both of pines and birches'; and then he will come and give us a look up in Corrynakiegh. And if he does not, the devil may take him, for what I care."

"But would it not be simpler," I asked, "to write him a few words in black and white?"

"It would certainly be much simpler for me to write to him, but it would be a sore job for John to read it. He would have to go to school for two-three years; and it's possible we might be wearied waiting for him."

So that night Alan carried down his fiery cross and set it in John's window.

About noon the next day we spied a man straggling up the open side of the mountain in the sun, and looking

round him as he came. No sooner had Alan seen him than he whistled; the man turned and came a little towards us: then Alan would give another "peep!" and the man would come still nearer.

He was a ragged, bearded man about forty, and looked both simple-minded and savage. Alan wanted him to carry a spoken message to James; but John said, "I would forget it."

We lacked the means of writing, but Alan was a man of resources; he searched the wood until he found the quill of a dove, which he shaped into a pen; made himself a kind of ink with gunpowder and water; and tearing a corner from his French military commission, he sat down and wrote:

DEAR KINSMAN,—Please send the money by the bearer to the place he knows of.

Your affectionate cousin,

A. S.

John was three full days gone, but about five in the evening of the third, we heard a whistling in the wood, which Alan answered; and soon the man came up the waterside, looking for us.

He gave us the news of the country: that it was alive with red-coats; that weapons were being found, and poor folk brought in trouble daily; and that James and some of his servants were already in prison. It seemed it was said on all sides that Alan Breck had fired the shot; and there was a bill issued for both him and me, with one hundred pounds reward.

The little note John had carried us from Mrs. Stewart asked Alan not to let himself be captured, assuring him, if he fell in the hands of the troops, both he and James were dead men. The money she had sent was all that she could beg or borrow. It was less than five guineas, more than I had, but he had to get as far as France, and I only to Queensferry.

"It's little enough," said Alan, putting the purse in his pocket, "but it'll do. And now, John Breck, if ye will hand me over my button, this gentleman and me will be for taking the road."

Doing so, John took himself off by one way; and Alan and I (getting our goods together) struck into another to resume our escape.

After a night of hard travelling, we lay down in a thick bush of heather to sleep. Alan took the first watch; and it seemed to me I had scarce closed my eyes before I was shaken up to take the second. We had no clock to go by; and Alan stuck a sprig of heath in the ground to serve instead; so that as soon as the shadow of the bush should fall so far to the east, I might know to rouse him. But I was by this time so weary that I could have slept twelve hours; my joints slept even when my mind was waking; the hot smell of the heather, and the drone of the wild bees, were like a cup of warm milk to me; and every now and again I would give a jump and find I had been dozing.

The last time I woke I seemed to have come back from farther away, and thought the sun had taken a great start in the heavens. I looked at the sprig of heath, and at that I could have cried aloud: for I saw I had betrayed my trust. My head was nearly turned with fear and shame; and at what I saw, when I looked out around me on the moor, my heart sank. For sure enough, horse-soldiers had come down during my sleep, and were drawing near to us, fanned out and riding their horses to and fro in the deep parts of the heather.

When I waked Alan, he glanced first at the soldiers, then at the mark and the position of the sun, and knitted his brows with a sudden, quick look.

"What are we to do now?" I asked.

"We'll have to play at being hares," said he. "Do you see that mountain?" pointing to one.

"Ay," said I.

"Well, then," said he, "let us strike for that."

"But, Alan, that will take us across the very coming of the soldiers."

"I know that," said he; "but if we are driven back on Appin, we are two dead men. So now, David man, be brisk!"

With that he began to run forward on his hands and knees with an incredible quickness. All the time he kept winding in and out in the lower parts of the moorland where we were best concealed.

I had awakened just in time.

At length, in the first gloaming of the night, we heard a trumpet sound, and looking back from among the heather, saw the troop beginning to collect. A little after, they had built a fire and camped for the night.

At this I begged that we might lie down and sleep.

"There shall be no sleep tonight," said Alan. "We got

through in the nick of time, and shall we hazard what we've gained? No, no, when the day comes, it shall find you and me in a safe place on the mountain."

"Lead away," said I. "I'll follow."

By daylight, we were able to walk upon our feet like men, instead of crawling like brutes. However, he must have been as stupid with weariness as myself, or we should not have walked into an ambush like blind men. It fell in this way. We were going down a heathery valley, when upon a sudden three or four ragged men leaped out, and the next moment we were lying on our backs, each with a knife at his throat.

I then heard Alan and another whispering in Gaelic; and the knives were put away.

"They are Cluny's men," said Alan. "We couldn't have fallen better."

Now Cluny Macpherson, the chief of the Vourich clan, had been one of the leaders of the great rebellion six years before; there was a price on his life; and I had supposed him long ago in France.

"What," I cried, "is Cluny still here?"

"Ay, is he so!" said Alan. "Still in his own country, and kept by his own clan. King George can do no more."

I was so tired I had to be carried by Cluny's men into the glens and hollows and into the heart of that dismal mountain hideout.

Alan and I remained a few days, gaining our strength, before going on. Cluny's men put us across the Loch Errocht under cloud of night, and we went down its eastern shore to another hiding-place near the head of Loch Rannoch. From there we got us up into the tops of the mountains, and for the best part of three nights headed for the lowlands by Kippen. There were troops in every district, and this route led us through the country of Alan's blood-foes, the Glenorchy Campbells.

By day we lay and slept in the drenching heather; by night, we clambered upon break-neck hills. We often wandered; we were often so involved in fog, that we must lie quiet till it lightened. A fire was never to be thought of. Our only food was drammach and a portion of cold meat we had carried from Cluny's; and as for drink, we had plenty of water.

The third night we were to pass through the western end of the country of Balquhidder. I was dead weary, deadly sick and full of pains and shiverings; the chill of the wind went through me. At last I put my pride away from me, and declared, "Alan, if you cannot help me, I must just die here." I spoke in a weeping voice that would have melted a heart of stone.

"Can you walk?" asked Alan.

"No," said I, "not without help. This last hour my legs have been fainting under me; I've a stitch in my side like a red-hot iron; I can't breathe right."

"Let me get my arm around you," he said; "that's the way. Now lean upon me. God knows where there's a house! We're in Balquhidder. We'll follow down the creek, where there's bound to be houses. My poor man!"

At the door of the first house we came to, Alan knocked. Chance served us very well, for it was a household of Maclarens, and the Maclarens followed Alan's chief in war. Alan was not only welcome for his name's sake but known by reputation. Here then I was got to bed without delay, and a doctor fetched, who found me in a very sorry plight. But whether because he was a very good doctor, or I a very young, strong man, I lay bedridden for no more than a week, and before a month I was able to take the road again with a good heart.

It was already far through August, and beautiful warm weather, with every sign of an early and great harvest, when I was pronounced able for my journey. Our money was now run so low that we must think first of all on speed; for if we came not soon to the lawyer Mr. Rankeillor's, or if when we came there he should fail to help me, we must surely starve. In Alan's view, besides, the hunt for us must have now greatly slackened; and the line of the Forth and even Stirling Bridge, which is the main pass over that river, would be watched with little interest.

"It's a chief principle in military affairs," said he, "to go where you are least expected."

The first night, accordingly, we pushed to the house of a Maclaren in Strathire, where we slept, and from there we set forth again about the fall of night to make another easy stage. The next day we lay in a heather bush on the hillside in Uam Var, within view of a herd of deer, the happiest ten hours of sleep in a fine, breathing sunshine and bone-dry ground, that I have ever tasted. That night we reached Allan Water, and followed it down; and coming to the edge of the hills saw the whole Carse* of Stirling underfoot, with the town and the castle on a hill in the midst of it, and the moon shining on the Links of Forth.

"Now," said Alan, "you're in your own land again. We passed the Highland Line in the first hour; and now if we could but pass that crooked water, we might cast our bonnets in the air."

I was for pushing straight across; but Alan was more wary.

"It looks too quiet," said he; "but for all that we'll lie down here behind a dyke, and make sure."

At last there came by an old, hobbling woman with a crutch. The woman was so little, and the night so dark, that we soon lost sight of her; only heard the sound of her steps, and her stick, and a cough that she had by fits.

And just then—"Who goes?" cried a voice, and we heard the butt of a musket rattle on the bridgestones. I must suppose the guard had been sleeping, so that had we tried, we might have passed unseen; but he was awake now.

"This'll never do for us, David," said Alan.

And without another word, he began to crawl away through the fields.

"Well?" said I.

"Well," said Alan, "what would you have us do? They're not the fools I took them for. We have still the Forth to pass, Davie, and if we cannot pass the river, we'll have to see what we can do for the firth."

"But a river can be swum."

"By them that have the skill of it," returned he, "I have yet to hear that either you or me is much of a swimmer."

*Carse is low, rich land, usually along a river, in this case the Forth River.

"But if it's hard to pass a river, it stands to reason it must be worse to pass a sea."

"But there's such a thing as a boat," said Alan.

By the next night, we had borrowed a boat from an innkeeper's kindly daughter, and we rowed across, setting down on the Lothian shore.

CHAPTER 10
I Come to Mr. Rankeillor

T HE NEXT DAY, it was agreed that Alan should fend for himself till sunset; but as soon as it began to grow dark, he should lie in the fields by the roadside, and not stir until he heard me whistling. He taught me a little fragment of a Highland air, which has run in my head from that day to this. Every time it comes to me, it takes me off to that last day of my uncertainty, with Alan sitting up in the bottom of the den, whistling and beating the measure with a finger, and the gray of dawn coming on his face.

I was in the long street of Queensferry before the sun was up. It was a fairly built town, the houses of good stone, and I was ashamed of my tattered clothes.

As the morning went on, and the people began to appear out of the houses, I saw now that I had no clear proof of my rights over my uncle's. It might be no easy matter even to come to meet with the lawyer, far less to convince him of my story. I went up and down, and through the street, and down to the harbor-side. At last I chanced to have stopped in front of a very good house, from which came out a red-faced, kindly, important-looking man in a powdered wig and spectacles. This gentleman was so much struck with my poor appearance that he came straight up to me and asked me what I wanted.

I told him I was come to Queensferry on business, and asked him to direct me to the house of Mr. Rankeillor.

"Why," said he, "that is his house that I have just come out of; and for a rather surprising chance, I am that very man."

"Then, sir," said I, "I have to beg the favor of an interview. My name is David Balfour."

"And where have you come from, Mr. Balfour?"

"A great many strange places, sir."

He led me back into his house, cried out to someone whom I could not see that he would be busy all morning, and brought me into his little dusty chamber full of books and documents.

"I have reason to believe myself some rights on the estate of Shaws," I told him.

He asked me of where and when I was born, and of my parents, and finally, "Have you any papers proving who you are?"

"No, sir," said I, "but they are in the hands of Mr. Campbell, the minister. For that matter, I do not think my uncle Mr. Ebenezer Balfour would deny me."

"Did you ever meet a man of the name of Hoseason?" he asked.

"I did so, sir," said I; "for it was by his means and by pay of my uncle, that I was kidnapped within sight of this town, carried to sea, suffered shipwreck and a hundred other hardships, and stand before you today in these poor clothes."

"You were kidnapped? In what sense?"

"In the plain meaning of the word, sir," said I. "I was on

my way to your house, when I was kidnapped on board the brig, cruelly struck down, thrown below, and knew no more of anything till we were far at sea. I was destined for the plantations; a fate that I have escaped."

"The brig *Covenant* was lost on June the 27th," said he, looking in his book, "and we are now at August the 24th. Here is a considerable gap, Mr. Balfour, of nearly two months."

"Before I tell my story, I would be glad to know that I was talking to a friend," I said. "You are not to forget, sir, that I have already suffered by my trustfulness; and was shipped off to be a slave by the very man that is your employer."

"I *was* indeed your uncle's lawyer," he said. "But while you were gallivanting, a good deal of water has run under the bridges. On the very day of your sea disaster, your friend the minister Mr. Campbell stalked into my office, demanding you. I had never heard of you; but I had known your father. Mr. Ebenezer admitted having seen you; declared that he had given you much money; and that you had started for the continent of Europe. I am not exactly sure that anyone believed him," continued Mr. Rankeillor with a smile; "and in particular he so disliked my own suspicions, he fired me. Shortly thereafter, comes Captain Hoseason with the story of your drowning."

Thereupon I told him my story from the start. When I mentioned Alan Breck, we had an odd scene. The name of Alan had of course rung through Scotland, with the news of the Appin murder, and the offer of a reward; and his name had no sooner escaped me than the lawyer said, "We will call your friend, if you please, Mr. Thomson."

By this I saw he had already guessed I might be coming to the murder.

"Well, well," said the lawyer, when I had quite done, "this is a great Odyssey of yours. This Mr. Thomson seems

to me a gentleman of some choice qualities, though perhaps a little bloody-minded. But you are doubtless quite right to stick to him; he stuck to you. He was your true companion. Well, well, I think you are near the end of your troubles."

He had another plate set at his table for my dinner, and provided for me water, soap, and a comb; and laid out some clothes that belonged to his son. I made what change I could in my appearance.

When I had done, Mr. Rankeillor said, "Sit down, Mr. David, and now that you are looking a little more like yourself, you will be wondering, no doubt, about your father and uncle. It is a strange tale, and the matter hinges on a love affair."

"Truly," said I, "I cannot very well join that notion with my uncle."

"But your uncle, Mr. David, was not always old," replied the lawyer, "and not always ugly. He had a fine, gallant air. In 1715 he ran away to join the rebels.* It was your father that pursued him, found him in a ditch, and brought him back. The two lads fell in love, and with the same lady. The end of it was, your mother preferred your father. Your uncle complained so loudly, so selfishly, that your father gave over his estate to Ebenezer, and took the lady. Now your father should have consulted his lawyer, myself, as this action was unjust. Your father and mother lived and died poor folk; and, in the meanwhile, what a time it has been for the tenants on the estate of the Shaws! Money was all Mr. Ebenezer got by his bargain. He was selfish when he was young, he is selfish now that he is old."

"Well, sir," said I, "and in all this, what is my position?"

"The estate is yours, beyond a doubt," replied the lawyer. "It matters nothing what your father signed, you are the lawful heir to the estate. My advice, however, is to make a very easy bargain with your uncle, perhaps even leaving him at Shaws, and contenting yourself till he dies with a fair sum."

I told him I was very willing to be easy, and began to see the outlines of that scheme on which we afterwards acted.

"The surest way to make the bargain," I asked, "is to get him to admit the kidnapping?"

"Surely," said Mr. Rankeillor.

"Well, sir," said I, "here is my plan."

Having told it to him, and obtained his liking for it, we set out from the house to meet with Alan, "Mr. Thomson." Mr. Rankeillor's clerk, Torrance, followed behind with a deed in his pocket, and a covered basket in his hand. All

---

*In 1715, there was a Jacobite rising in support of James Francis Edward Stuart, father of Charles Stuart and the son and heir of James II of England.

through the town the lawyer was bowing right and left, and being stopped by gentlemen on matters of town or private business. At last we were clear of the houses, and began to go along towards the Hawes Inn and the Ferry pier, the scene of my misfortune. I could not look upon the place without emotion, recalling how many that had been with me that day were now no more. All these, and the brig herself, I had outlived.

I was so thinking when, all of a sudden, Mr. Rankeillor cried out, clapped his hand to his pockets, and began to laugh. "Why, I have forgot my glasses!"

At that, I knew that he had left his spectacles at home on purpose, so that he might have the benefit of Alan's help without the legal awkwardness of recognizing him. For how could Rankeillor swear to my friend's identity?

As soon as we were past the Hawes, Mr. Rankeillor walked behind with Torrance and sent me forward as scout. I went up the hill, whistling from time to time the tune Alan had taught me; and at length I had the pleasure to hear it answered and to see Alan rise from behind a bush. At the mere sight of my clothes, he began to brighten up; and as soon as I had told him my plan, he was a new man.

I cried and waved on Mr. Rankeillor, who came up alone and was presented to my friend, Mr. Thomson.

Night was quite come when we came in view of the house of Shaws. It was dark and mild, with a pleasant, rustling wind that covered the sound of our approach; and as we drew near we saw no glimmer of light in the building. It seemed my uncle was already in bed, which was indeed the best thing for our arrangements. We made our last whispered plans some fifty yards away; and then the lawyer and Torrance and I crept quietly up and crouched down beside the corner of the house; and as soon as we were in our places, Alan strode to the door and began to knock.

At last we could hear the noise of a window gently thrust up, and knew that my uncle had come to his observatory. By what light there was, he would see Alan standing, like a dark shadow, on the steps; the three witnesses were hidden quite out of his view.

"What's this?" said he. "This is no kind of time of night for decent folk; I have no dealings with nighthawks. What brings you here? I have a gun."

"Is that you, Mr. Balfour?" returned Alan. "Have a care with that musket."

"What brings you here? and who are you?"

"I have no desire to shout my name to the countryside," said Alan; "but what brings me here is another story, being more your affair than mine."

"And what is it?"

"David," said Alan.

"What was that?" cried my uncle. "I'll come right down." He shut the window, and at last, we heard, downstairs, the creak of the door hinges.

"And now," said my uncle, "mind that I have my gun, and if you take a step nearer you're as good as dead."

"A very polite speech," said Alan, "to be sure."

"No," said my uncle, "but I'm bound to be prepared. And now you'll name your business."

"I am a Highland gentleman," said Alan. "My name has no business in my story; but the county of my friends is not very far from the Isle of Mull, of which you will have heard. It seems there was a ship lost in those parts; and the next day a gentleman of my family was seeking wreckwood for his fire along the sands, when he came upon a lad that was half drowned. Well, he brought him to; and he and some other gentlemen took and locked him in an old, ruined castle, where from that day to this he has been a great expense to my friends. My friends are a wee wild-like, and not so particular about the law; and finding that the lad was your born nephew, Mr. Balfour, they asked me to give you a call and talk. And I may tell you, unless we can agree upon some terms, you are little likely to set eyes upon him. For my friends are not very well off."

My uncle cleared his throat. "I'm not very caring," said he. "He wasn't a good lad, and I've no call to interfere."

"Ay, ay," said Alan, "I see what you're at: pretending you don't care, to make the ransom smaller."

"No," said my uncle, "it's the simple truth. I take no manner of interest in the lad, and I'll pay no ransom, and you can do what you like with him, for what I care."

"Hoot, sir," said Alan. "Blood's thicker than water! You cannot desert your brother's son; and if you did, and it came to be known, you wouldn't be a very popular man."

"I'm not just very popular the way it is," returned Ebenezer; "and I don't see how it would come to be known. Not by me, anyway; nor yet by you or your friends."

"Then it'll have to be David that tells it," said Alan.

"How's that?"

"Oh, just this way," said Alan. "My friends would doubt-less keep your nephew as long as there was any likelihood of silver to be made of it, but if there was none, I am sure they would let him go where he pleased. There are two ways of it, Mr. Balfour: either you liked David and would pay to get him back; or else you had very good reasons for not wanting him, and would pay for us to keep him. It seems it's not the first; well then, it's the second; and as I see it, it should be a pretty penny in my pocket and the pockets of my friends."

"I don't follow you there," said my uncle.

"No?" said Alan. "Well, see here: you don't want the lad back; well, what do you want done with him, and how much will you pay?"

My uncle made no answer, but shifted uneasily.

"Come, sir," cried Alan. "I would have you know that I am a gentleman, not a servant to be kept waiting. Answer me in civility, or by the top of Glencoe, I will ram three feet of iron through you."

"Just tell me about how much silver you'll want," said my uncle, "and you'll see if we can agree."

"Do you want the lad killed or kept?" asked Alan.

"O, sir," cried Ebenezer. "That's no kind of language!"

"Killed or kept!" repeated Alan.

"O, kept, kept!" wailed my uncle. "We'll have no bloodshed, if you please."

"Well," said Alan, "as you please; that'll cost more."

"More?" cried Ebenezer. "Would you stain your hands with crime?"

"Hoot!" said Alan. "They're both crimes! And the killing's easier, and quicker, and surer. Keeping the lad will be a troublesome job."

"I'll have him kept, though," returned my uncle. "I'm a man of principle, and if I have to pay for it, I'll have to pay for it."

"Well, well," said Alan, "and now about the price. It's not very easy for me to set a name upon it; I would have to know some small matters. I would have to know, for instance, what you gave Hoseason?"

"To Hoseason? What for?" cried my uncle.

"For kidnapping David," said Alan.

"It's a lie, a lie!" cried my uncle. "He was never kidnapped. He lied in his throat that told you that. Kidnapped? He never was!"

"What did you pay him?"

"Has Hoseason told you himself?"

"How else could I know?"

"Well," said my uncle, "I don't care what he said, he lied, and the solemn truth is this, that I gave him twenty pounds. But I'll be perfectly honest with you: for with that, he was

to have the price of the lad in Carolina, which would be as much more, but not from my pocket, you see."

"Thank you, Mr. Thomson," said the lawyer, stepping forward, "that will do excellently. Good-evening, Mr. Balfour."

And, "Good-evening, Uncle Ebenezer," said I.

And, "It's a fine night, Mr. Balfour," added Torrance.

Never a word said my uncle; but just sat where he was on the top doorstep and stared upon us like a man turned to stone. Alan took away his gun; and the lawyer, taking him by the arm, plucked him up from the doorstep, led him into the kitchen, where we all followed, and set him down in a chair beside the hearth.

"Come, come, Mr. Ebenezer," said the lawyer, "you must not be down-hearted, for I promise you we shall make easy terms." Mr. Rankeillor and my uncle passed into the next chamber to consult. They stayed there about an hour; at the end of which period they had come to a good understanding, and my uncle and I set our hands to the agreement in a formal manner. By the terms of this, my uncle bound himself to pay me two-thirds of the yearly income of Shaws.

So the beggar had come home; and when I lay down that night on the kitchen chests, I was a man of means and had a name in the country. Alan and Torrance and Rankeillor slept and snored on their hard beds; but for me who had lain out under heaven and upon dirt and stones, so many days and nights, and often with an empty belly, and in fear of death, I lay till dawn, looking at the fire and planning my future.

The next day Mr. Rankeillor supplied me with money and letters of introduction to his bankers and to the Advocate, whom I owed testimony about the murder. While Mr. Rankeillor and Torrance set out for the Ferry, Alan and I turned for the city of Edinburgh. As we went by the footpath and beside the gateposts, we kept looking back at the house of my fathers. It stood there, bare and great and smokeless, like a place not lived in.

Alan and I went slowly forward upon our way, having little heart either to walk or speak. The same thought was uppermost in both, that we were near the time of our parting; and remembrance of all the bygone days sat upon us sorely. We talked indeed of what should be done; and it was resolved that Alan should keep to the county, biding now here, now there, but coming once in the day to the particular place where I might be able to communicate with him. In the meanwhile, I was to seek out a lawyer, who was an Appin Stewart, and a man therefore to be wholly trusted; and it should be his part to find a ship and arrange for Alan's safe departure. No sooner was this business done, than the words seemed to leave us.

We came the by-way over the hill of Corstorphine; and when we got near to the place called Rest-and-be-Thankful, and looked down on bogs and over to the city and the castle on the hill, we both stopped, for we both knew

without a word said that we had come to where our ways parted. I gave him what money I had, and then we stood a while, and looked over at Edinburgh in silence.

"Well, good-bye," said Alan, and held out his hand.

"Good-bye," said I, and gave the hand a little grasp, and went off down hill.

Neither one of us looked the other in the face, nor so long as he was in my view did I take one back glance at the friend I was leaving. But as I went on my way to the city, I felt so lost and lonesome, that I could have found it in my heart to sit down by the dyke, and cry and weep like any baby.

It was coming near noon when I passed in by the West Kirk and the Grassmarket into the streets of the capital. And yet all the time I was thinking of Alan, and all the time there was a cold gnawing in my inside like a remorse for something wrong.

The hand of fate brought me in my drifting to the very doors of the bank.